"Even now you do not trust me not to allow you to be pushed aside."

"You've got your plans." Shrugging, Kayla looked away. "You're on a schedule."

"Plans that include marriage and a family." Was she still not getting it?

"Yes." This time the word sounded torn from her, not annoyed, but pained.

Again. Still. It did not matter which.

Andreas wanted that pain gone. Now. "There is a simple solution to both our dilemmas."

"You think so?" She was looking at him again, her eyes molten silver and blazing with anger.

Anger he did not understand, but was just as determined to extinguish as the pain. "I know it."

"What is this *simple solution*?" Her concrete disbelief in him having *any* solution that would appease her was written into every lovely aspect of her face.

He would prove his problem-solving skills were up to the task. "Marry me."

USA TODAY bestselling author **Lucy Monroe** lives and writes in the gorgeous Pacific Northwest. While she loves her home, she delights in experiencing different cultures and places in her travels, which she happily shares with her readers through her books. A lifelong devotee of the romance genre, Lucy can't imagine a more fulfilling career than writing the stories in her head for her readers to enjoy.

Books by Lucy Monroe

Harlequin Presents

Million Dollar Christmas Proposal
Not Just the Greek's Wife
Heart of a Desert Warrior

Ruthless Russians

An Heiress for His Empire
A Virgin for His Prize

The Chatsfield

Sheikh's Scandal

By His Royal Decree

One Night Heir
Prince of Secrets

Royal Brides

The Prince's Virgin Wife
His Royal Love-Child
The Scorsolini Marriage Bargain
Forbidden: The Billionaire's Virgin Princess
Hired: The Sheikh's Secretary Mistress
For Duty's Sake

Visit the Author Profile page
at Harlequin.com for more titles.

Lucy Monroe

KOSTAS'S CONVENIENT BRIDE

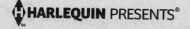

Recycling programs for this product may not exist in your area.

ISBN-13: 978-1-335-41932-3

Kostas's Convenient Bride

First North American publication 2018

Printed in U.S.A.

www.Harlequin.com

KOSTAS'S CONVENIENT BRIDE

For a UK reader who has become a long-distance friend, Catherine Bent. Thank you for reading my books, for caring about my characters and for sharing my obsession with BC as well as many smiles. Meeting you in Edinburgh was a highlight of our trip to Scotland and your boys are delightful!

CHAPTER ONE

KAYLA JONES HOP-RUSHED from the computer lab toward Andreas's office, buckling her denim wedge sandal as she went. She'd stripped out of her clean-room bunny suit in less than a minute, but re-dressing took longer.

Late for a high-priority meeting with the type A, ultra-alpha president of KJ Software was nothing Kayla wanted to be.

Even if he was her business partner. Technically.

He'd been weird lately. Cranky. Even more exacting than usual.

Andreas's twentysomething, superefficient male admin made a stopping motion with his hand. Kayla stopped but let her own widened eyes let him know how little she wanted to.

I know, he mouthed, sympathy imbuing his expression as some complicated sign language finally clued Kayla in to the fact that her peach cardigan knit jacket was on inside out.

She flipped it with rushed, jerky movements and then Bradley waved Kayla through with a significant nod toward her waistband. She looked down and realized the button at the top of the zipper on her peach damask-on-denim skirt was undone.

With a harried smile of thanks, she quickly fastened

it as she opened the door to the big man's office. "Sorry I'm late, Andreas, I was supervising tests on Dolphin." She preferred to name all their projects after marine life, and Andreas indulged her whimsy.

Kayla stopped abruptly as she realized her boss wasn't in his usual spot behind his big chrome-and-glass desk, but sitting at one end of the eight-person smoky-glass-topped meeting table.

A woman was with him. Blond hair piled in a sleek, professional updo and wearing a stylish white suit, she gave Kayla an assessing look.

"This is your business partner?" she asked Andreas, her tone tinged with disbelief.

"Yes." Andreas frowned at Kayla. "I told you this meeting was high priority."

"Technically, my smartphone told me. You flagged it." Who was this woman and what kind of meeting were they having?

Andreas gave her that look, the one that said Kayla was being a tad too literal again. She stifled the urge to apologize. She'd been working on that.

Not apologizing for being herself.

"Well, she's here now," the woman pointed out. "I presume we can get started now?" Her words were take-charge, but her expression toward Andreas was nothing but deferential.

"Get started on what?" Kayla asked as she settled into one of the leather high-backed chairs on Andreas's left, across from the stranger.

Apparently, he wasn't done glowering about Kayla's tardiness, because he did not answer.

Kayla rolled her eyes, absolutely refusing to utter the "I'm sorry" on the tip of her tongue. While he had marked the meeting as a priority, he'd had Bradley insert it into Kayla's schedule when she'd already blocked off the time prior for the Dolphin tests. She could wait out Andreas's snit. She'd done it before.

With a sound of impatience, the woman spoke. "We are here to discuss how Andreas's search for a wife will impact his business."

Everything around Kayla came into sharp focus. The sound each of them made as they breathed in the quiet of the room. The floral musk of the other woman's perfume that smelled out of place. The fingerprint smudges on the glass in front of the blonde that indicated she'd pressed her hands on the table for some reason. Kayla wanted to wipe them away, erase the evidence of the woman's presence, even as she sat there.

Kayla shook her head. Denial a scream inside her. That could not be right.

Andreas was no help. He still sat there with his stony "you were late" expression on his handsome, angular face, his green eyes snapping with disapproval.

"Search for a wife?" Kayla's breath ran out on the final word, her entire body going cold and then hot with the implications.

Andreas finally deigned to nod, not one strand of his dark hair going out of place with the short movement. "It's time."

"It is?" Kayla hadn't noticed Andreas being any less focused on business. Any more open to interpersonal relationships.

She would have noticed. She'd been watching for just such a change in him for the past six years.

In fact, lately, he'd been more driven and working even longer hours than usual and expecting her to do the same, wanting Dolphin's launch on time and without a single hiccup.

"I've exceeded my father's net worth. A wife and family are next on the list." He didn't shrug, his perfectly tailored suit-clad shoulders remaining ramrod straight, but the sense of dismissal was there in his voice.

Like this decision wasn't something life changing, monumental and the one thing Kayla had been hoping for since they broke up to become business partners.

Kayla looked at the woman who had informed her of Andreas's plans. Who was she? And why did she know Andreas's personal plans when Kayla, a friend, had not?

A truly horrifying prospect popped into Kayla's mind. Was this woman a matchmaker? It would be just like Andreas to hire a professional to find him a wife.

Not that he needed one.

While Kayla had been practically celibate the past few years, the same could not be said of Andreas. He'd taken many beautiful women to his bed, each and every one a risk to Kayla's hopes for the future. But he'd never gotten serious, his heart and Kayla's deepest desires remaining unchanged.

"That's what I'm here for," the sleek blonde said confidently, clearly thrilled to have a client of Andreas's stature on her roster.

"You're a matchmaker?" Kayla asked for confirmation, still trying to come to terms with that possible reality.

The woman nodded. "I own the Patterson Group."

It sounded like a firm of lawyers, not a service designed to bring people together in wedded bliss.

"She specializes in millionaires," Andreas added, like that was important.

"You're a billionaire." On paper anyway.

KJ Software was obscenely successful, just like Andreas had said it would be. The company, of which he owned 95 percent, was valued at over a billion dollars. Not bad for six years of blood, sweat and sleepless nights working.

The matchmaker nodded, her expression showing how much she appreciated the distinction and the fact Andreas was *her* client. Kayla knew being a billionaire rather than just worth millions mattered to Andreas too. A lot. That valuation was what had spurred this particular move toward domestic harmony, after all. He was finally worth more than his father, but still had more to prove.

Andreas was giving *Kayla* that look again. "Don't be so literal. The point is Miss Patterson—"

"Genevieve, please." The blonde's smile was all polish, no substance.

"Genevieve..."

Kayla wondered if Genevieve noticed the short pause and the way Andreas's square jaw tightened when using the more personal address. "...specializes in matching wealthy men with women who will make them the ideal wife."

Kayla was appalled and made no effort to hide it. "I don't think it works like that."

She wasn't opposed to matchmakers, was sure that there were plenty in the business who really believed in matching two people meant to be together, but this woman? She was every bit as predatory in her way as Andreas. Kayla had learned to read people very young.

If she hadn't, she wouldn't have survived her childhood.

Genevieve of the Patterson Group did not read as caring about long-term *happiness* or *emotional harmony* by any stretch of the imagination.

"My track record speaks for itself," the woman said now, superiority in her tone and the tilt of her head. So, impressed and happy to have Andreas as a client, but arrogant and utterly sure of herself, as well.

"If it didn't, I wouldn't consider your twenty-five-thousand-dollar retainer."

Kayla gasped. "I'm pretty sure you can buy a bride who looks like a supermodel for that kind of money."

Or, you know, marry the woman who had loved him for the last eight years and waited in hope for the past six.

"Your employer isn't looking for a trophy bride, he's interested in finding someone to share his life with." The matchmaker's self-righteous rhetoric would be a lot more convincing if she'd protested as vehemently at Andreas referring to finding a wife as the next item on his goal list.

If Andreas was really looking for a soul mate, he wouldn't look beyond the one woman he'd called friend for nearly a decade. Would he?

They hadn't broken up because they weren't good together. They'd ended their sexual relationship because Andreas had very strict views in regard to business and personal relationships. They'd never had what one might term a *romantic* relationship.

It had been friends with benefits.

Kayla had thought that was changing, that their relationship was morphing into something deeper.

She had been wrong.

Andreas had wanted to morph it all right, but not into something *more* personal. He'd wanted her senior project software design as the cornerstone for his new digital security company. And he'd made it very clear that he valued her skills as a programmer above her willingness to share his bed.

The six-year-old rejection she'd thought dealt with and dormant erupted with the power to leave her heart in ashes.

She had to get out of there.

Forcing her emotions behind the blank face she'd carefully crafted during a childhood bouncing from one foster home to another, Kayla asked, "Why am I here? What do you need from me?"

"You are my business partner," Andreas said, like that explained everything.

"Five-percent ownership hardly makes me a material partner." It was an old argument, one Andreas had never given in on.

The expression on the matchmaker's face said she agreed with Kayla, though.

Andreas frowned. The man didn't like being corrected and barely tolerated it from Kayla, but she never let that stop her from saying what needed saying. At least when it came to the business.

"You *are* my partner and this change in circumstance will affect the business and therefore you, by default." Andreas's tone brooked no argument.

Kayla was still confused, though, something she was used to when it came to interpersonal relationships, but not their company. "Why?"

She wasn't in the running. This whole "pay a matchmaker ridiculous amounts of money" thing made that very clear. And it hurt. Badly.

But she was confident Andreas had no clue. So, *why* was he so convinced Kayla's life was going to be impacted?

Once again, he was giving her a look that said she'd

missed something. Since he'd missed the fact she'd been in love with him since the beginning, she didn't feel as badly about that as she usually would have.

Genevieve spoke, her tone one you might use with a small child. "Marriage brings about significant changes in a person's life and since Andreas is the heart and blood of this company, it stands to reason his marriage will have a significant impact on the company and its higher-level employees."

Andreas's eyelid twitched at the familiar address, or maybe it was the reference to employees rather than partners, but he didn't correct Genevieve.

"Are we going public, then?" They'd been discussing it, or at least Andreas had been telling her he was thinking about it for the past year.

Doing so would make him a billionaire for real, not just net worth. Kayla wouldn't do badly out of it either. She'd be able to fund an entire chain of Kayla for Kids facilities, instead of the single local group home for foster children, with neighborhood after-school activities, she currently did.

"No." Andreas frowned. "I answer to no one."

Now, *that* didn't surprise her. While she might have dreams of funding Kayla for Kids houses in every major city, she knew how unlikely that really was. Andreas did not want to answer to shareholders, or a board of directors. His father had dictated things about Andreas's life when he'd had no way to stop the overbearing Greek tycoon, and no way would her Greek-American business mogul *ever* tolerate someone else having major say in his life again.

"Perhaps you should consider selling the company outright as you spoke about at our first meeting. It would free you up to make your search for the right marital partner," Genevieve suggested, her tone implying she thought it an imminently practical solution. "Being a liquid billionaire wouldn't hurt your chances in the dating pool either. I'm sure we could snag you royalty."

So much for *not* looking for a trophy wife.

Kayla couldn't get a full breath. "You want him to sell the company?" So he could *buy a princess*?

"It is one solution."

"To what?" So far, Kayla didn't see a problem that needed solving.

Except the whole *buy a bride* thing. And Andreas had plenty of money to do that without selling their company. Without ripping out from under her everything she'd spent the last six years building.

"Andreas cannot continue to put in twelve- to sixteen-hour days. It's part of the agreement with my firm." Genevieve tapped her tablet with one long fingernail.

"You signed an agreement?" Kayla asked Andreas.

He gave her that look. The one that implied she was a few steps behind in the business side of a discussion. It had happened before.

But this was crazy.

"That limits the number of hours you work?" she clarified.

"Yes."

"That doesn't mean you have to consider selling the company." Andreas wouldn't give in on this particular issue, would he? It was too important.

He might not love Kayla. Heck, maybe he'd never even really cared about her as anything but a brilliant programmer with a new idea, but he cared about their company. It wasn't just Kayla who'd found stability and a purpose with KJ Software.

Andreas had always been crazy protective when it came to the company and pure predator in his role as president. The idea that he would even consider selling it should be ludicrous. Only, the calculating expression in Andreas's green gaze made Kayla's short nails dig into suddenly sweaty palms.

No. He'd made comments over the past year. Sarcastic one-offs about selling KJ Software that she'd given the credence they deserved.

None.

Andreas might be the lifeblood of the company, but Genevieve had gotten it wrong. Kayla's job might technically be director of research and development, but she was KJ Software's *heart* and she couldn't be that when her own stopped beating. Didn't they realize that?

"Are you all right, Kayla?" Andreas asked, handsome features etched with concern.

She stared at him, not sure she could answer. Her entire world was imploding.

"We've done what we set out to do with this company." Andreas leaned back in his chair, his big body relaxed, his tone satisfied...like his words weren't slashing jagged wounds right into her heart. "Sebastian Hawk has approached me about a merger with his security firm."

"A merger or a buyout?" she demanded.

Andreas winced, perhaps recognizing his news was not as welcome as he'd expected it to be. "A buyout is the most likely final scenario."

"Why?" Owner of one of the largest security firms worldwide, Sebastian Hawk was one of their biggest customers and had been since the beginning. "He already licenses our software." For his own company and in a secondary capacity for his own clients.

Andreas replied, "He wants to own it."

"He's a control freak, like you."

Andreas shrugged. "He has three children and a legacy to leave them."

"What about your children?" Presumably if Andreas was ready to get married, he was looking forward to parenthood, as well.

He had often said the only reason he would ever marry was to have a real family. Didn't he want a legacy for his own children?

"I'm thinking about going into venture capital investments."

"You've been watching *that show* again, haven't you?" she asked, referring to a favorite reality television show of his.

They'd watched the show about venture capitalists who invested in and mentored start-up businesses together many times. Andreas prided himself on being able to guess which entrepreneurs were going to get multiple offers from the "sharks" and which would leave the "tank" without a single offer at all.

"As fascinating as all this is, we need to wrap this meeting up." Genevieve's voice grated in unwelcome reminder of her presence as she glanced at her designer watch. "I have another client meeting."

Really? Lots of superwealthy guys were looking for bride pimps? "How many clients do you take on at a time?"

"That is privileged information," Genevieve informed her haughtily.

But Kayla had spent most of her life in the foster

care system. Haughty wasn't going to intimidate her. "Not with the kind of retainer you charged Andreas."

"I was under the impression you paid out of your personal account?"

Andreas's expression filled with annoyance. "Of course I did."

"Then, I do not see where this is any of your business." The matchmaker's condescending tone might have annoyed Kayla, but she had concerns much closer to her heart right now.

She stood on shaky legs. "You're right. It's not. In fact, I still don't know what the heck I'm doing here at all. If you're going to sell the company, my tiny minority percent isn't going to stop you. If you want to pay this woman more than a lot of people make in a year to find you some dates when I don't see you struggling for company now, that's none of my business."

The cold inside her grew with every word, but so did Kayla's resolve. "I do not appreciate being called away from my work for something you could have handled in a text." *I'm hiring a matchmaker.*

"You expected me to tell you I was selling the company in a text?" Andreas demanded, sounding shocked.

"I didn't expect you to sell the company at all, certainly not to tell me about it as a fait accompli in a meeting with a third party." Dismissing Genevieve's presence, Kayla met Andreas's gaze. "But I'm realizing now I've been wrong about a lot of things."

He'd said this meeting was about the matchmaker. The selling of the company had come up as part of the discussion. Or that was how it had seemed. But apparently, it had been part of his agenda all along.

Kayla turned on her heel and walked out of the office, the numbness spreading with the cold. She'd been like this a few times before in her life.

The day she realized her mom was not coming back. She hadn't spoken for two years after.

The day her foster mom died and she was placed in the first of another string of homes.

The day she realized Andreas wanted her for her programming skills more than her place in his bed, or even their friendship.

Andreas's personal assistant stood up as Kayla came out of the office. "Are you okay?"

She just shook her head.

"What's going on?"

"He's getting married." Kayla wasn't going to mention the possibility he was going to sell their company. After all, that wasn't *supposed* to have been the reason for the meeting.

"To *her*?" Bradley's eyes widened, his face going slack.

"She's the matchmaker."

Bradley laid his hand on Kayla's arm. "I'm sorry."

He didn't say anything else, but he'd been working for Andreas from the beginning. Other than Andreas, Bradley knew Kayla better than anyone else alive. Maybe better, because he'd realized the first year they worked together that she was in love with the oblivious Greek.

CHAPTER TWO

A COUPLE OF hours later, Kayla was lost in the code of a program they'd scrapped the year before as unfeasible when a hand landed on her shoulder. She knew immediately whom that hand belonged to. "I'm busy, Andreas."

"You're not on a development team right now."

"I'm the director of research and development. That means I get to choose what projects I work on."

"So, what are you working on?"

"A program that will make Sebastian Hawk another hundred million if I can get it working."

"We haven't sold our company yet."

"But we are selling it."

"I don't know, are we?"

She spun around to face Andreas. "Don't play games with me, Andreas."

He sighed, running his fingers through his jet-black hair, his green eyes troubled. "Yes, we're selling."

"When were you going to tell me?" She wanted to scream, to rail at him and demand answers to how he could rip everything out from under her on one go, but she wouldn't.

For one thing, he wouldn't understand. The fact they were standing here having this conversation at all told her that. For another, if she let out some of the pain, it would all come out and she wasn't about to let that happen.

"After our meeting with Miss Patterson."

"Why did you pull me into that?"

"She wanted to ask you some questions."

"Why?" Kayla did her best to stop that one word coming out sounding like the pain-filled cry it was, but she could hear the ragged edges to her voice if he couldn't.

Andreas winced. "You're my closest friend."

"And she interviews your friends?" How invasive was that?

"Yes."

"What happened to separating personal from business?"

"We've managed to stay friends."

They had until today.

Did he have any idea how arrogant he sounded, or how hurtful his words were? No, of course he didn't. Andreas was so far removed from human feelings, it was scary sometimes.

"We're such good friends, you didn't bother to tell me you wanted to get married. That you'd hired some high-priced matchmaker to make it happen. You didn't talk over the plan with me, much less the plan to sell *our* company. Yeah, we're *great* friends." The sarcasm was so thick in her voice there was no way even Mr. Clueless himself could miss it.

"I did tell you about Genevieve." He frowned, completely ignoring the issue of KJ Software. "Today."

Kayla felt a headache coming on behind her left eye. "Friends talk about that kind of thing *before* they do it."

"How would you know?"

"I just do." She might not have a lot of friends, but she had more than he did. "I know how to be a friend."

His green gaze narrowed. "Are you saying I don't?"

"Unless it comes to throwing money at a problem, I'm going to go with no on this one."

"I'm going to pretend you didn't say that because I am aware you are upset over the sale of the company."

How magnanimous of him.

She rubbed her temple. It didn't help the growing headache. Only one thing would. Ending this conversation. "Bradley would have told me."

"I pay him well, but not enough to hire Genevieve Patterson's services. It would not have come up."

"He doesn't need them." When Bradley decided to settle down, he would do things the old-fashioned way. He'd look for someone he loved.

"Is that relevant?"

Her hand tightened around the stylus she'd been using to take notes. "To you? Probably not."

"Bradley is not my friend. He is my employee." Andreas grimaced.

"He'll figure that out right away when he finds out you're selling the company and making his position redundant."

"I plan to take Bradley with me."

She wasn't surprised, but looked into Andreas's green gaze for confirmation of his words. Her trust factor was at an all-time low with this man right now. "Into your venture capital firm?"

"Yes."

"Good." She wanted Bradley to be okay. And he worked well for Andreas.

Andreas smiled, that winner's grin. The one he used when he was sure things were going his way. "You'll

have enough from the sale of the company to partici-
pate materially in the new company."

"No." She'd made plans for the money going public
would give her. Changing the source of that windfall to
an outright sale wouldn't change her plans.

"We make a good team."

"No."

For the first time, Andreas looked disconcerted.
"You haven't even heard me out."

"There's nothing to hear. I'm not interested in changing careers. I love what I do and I plan to keep doing it."

"You'd start a new business in competition with
Hawk? Do I need to remind you that business is not
your strong suit?"

Oh, if she were a violent woman! He'd have a hand-
sized print on his cheek right now. Just to take that smug
look off his face. "No. *If* I wanted to start my own software development company, I'd find a partner. But I
don't see any reason to leave this one. Sebastian Hawk
respects my abilities and I'm sure he realizes that without me, the software development department would
be crippled."

Especially if she took the team with her.

"You have a high opinion of your abilities."

"You used to too."

"I still do."

She didn't reply to that. In fact, she was done talking. Kayla turned back to her computer and changed a
line of code before inserting the new series she'd written over the last hour.

"Kayla."

"Go away, Andreas."

"Genevieve wants to meet with you."

"I don't know why. Anything she needs to know, she can send me an email."

"I thought we could meet together."

Because that went so well the first time around. "Go away, Andreas."

If she kept saying it, he would eventually obey. Everyone did. Even Andreas.

He said her name again. She ignored him, putting in her earbuds and turning on her favorite work playlist. She began typing.

He stood behind her a lot longer than she expected, but after the second song, he was finally gone.

Kayla's shoulders sagged and her heart hurt in her chest.

She looked at the computer screen that had been designed to be unreadable by anyone not directly in front of it. It was filled with a series of lines that all said the same thing. "I need you to go away."

She carefully deleted the dozens of lines saying the same thing, but no matter how hard she tried, she could not get back into programming mode.

She needed to know what her future held, now that she realized it wasn't going to have Andreas Kostas in it.

She left her development station with the computer with no conduit to the internet and moved to her desk and tablet. It was a lot easier than she expected to find a flight to Sebastian Hawk's headquarters the following day.

Kayla marked herself as out of the building the next day, canceled the one meeting she had to attend and sent off two emails requesting coverage for the others she wouldn't be at.

Andreas swore as he read the gushing but uncompromising email from Genevieve telling him he had to fill out the entire personality and interests form before their next consultation. He'd thought the intake form had asked everything pertinent.

Apparently, the matchmaker did not agree.

If Kayla wasn't pissed at him, he could have asked for her help. As awkward as she could be socially because of her overly literal mind, she got stuff like this with surprising understanding.

The meeting between her and the matchmaker could have gone worse, but he wasn't sure how. Both he and Genevieve had gotten Kayla's back up.

It had been a couple of years since she'd tuned him out with earbuds. But when she did it, there was no point trying to communicate with her.

Kayla had a stubborn streak that could outlast his own when the issue mattered to her.

She was angry he'd decided to sell the company, that she'd learned today in the meeting.

Telling Genevieve his plans to sell before talking to Kayla had been a mistake. He could see that now.

He owed his partner more respect than that.

It was also clear that she believed as his friend, he should have talked to her about hiring the matchmaker ahead of time too.

He didn't see it.

If anything, Kayla should have realized this was the next step. She was the only person he'd ever shared his plans with, but he *had* shared them.

A long time ago, when their friendship had included sex and no business partnership.

He didn't like knowing she was upset with him. Kayla Jones was the only person whose opinion really mattered to him.

Breakfast apology éclairs might be in order tomorrow.

Hell, why not deal with it tonight and take her to dinner at that Vietnamese place she liked?

Kayla wasn't in the computer lab when he got there and didn't answer her phone when he called.

She was still ignoring him.

Too bad for her, he wasn't in the mood to be ignored.

He'd just go by her condo. It wasn't exactly a trip, a few floors below his penthouse that was double the size of her small one bedroom. At least she'd moved into his building and out of the hopeless apartment in an unacceptable part of town.

Forty-five minutes later, he sent a short text. Where the hell are you?

When she didn't reply in five minutes, he sent another one. I can keep this up all night until your damn phone's batteries die from all the alerts.

He was surprised when she didn't reply after that one. Andreas didn't make idle threats, though. He proceeded to blow her phone up with texts every five minutes, even more shocked when the first few did not elicit a response and moving into downright worried by the time his phone rang forty-five minutes and eight texts later.

"Stop!" Anger and exasperation warred in her shout.

More than a little annoyed himself, he demanded, *"Where are you?"*

"You're not my keeper."

Knowing he did not have to be worried for her safety allowed him to ratchet back on the irritation. He went for calm, rational. "We need to talk."

"Maybe you should have thought of that little thing before this minute, you think?"

"We would have talked this afternoon if you hadn't

thrown a hissy fit and stormed out of my office." Okay, maybe not so calm.

"That? Was not a hissy fit. I do not lose my cool, storm anywhere and I never throw fits, hissy or otherwise." *Oh, hell*. Her voice had gone cold and devoid of emotion, like it did when she was protecting herself.

He didn't like thinking she felt the need to protect herself from him. "Be reasonable, Kayla. You're blowing this all out of proportion."

"What exactly? The fact you're planning to take my home away because that wife pimp says you need to?"

"I'm not doing anything with your condo."

"Don't play the idiot!" Kayla's shout stunned him into silence.

She was right; she didn't lose her cool. The only time he'd ever heard her raise her voice was when they used to sleep together. And no matter how good a lover he was, the times she let herself go enough to scream were few. Allowing himself to remember their sexual past was not productive, as he had learned early on after taking her on as a business partner.

He could not afford that kind of distraction from his goals.

Right now, his goal was figuring out what was going on with his best friend. "Kayla?"

"I'm taking the day off tomorrow." The even tone of her voice after that primal scream of pain was almost worse than the shout itself.

"Why?"

"I have things to do."

"What things?"

"How did your wife pimp put it? None of your business, Andreas."

"Kayla, stop it. I don't know what has gotten into you—"

The low beep that indicated the call had been ended interrupted Andreas. Damn it. She should know he wouldn't sell the company without an after plan for *both* of them.

He hadn't expected her to want to go into venture capitalism herself, not really, but she was brilliant at computer code and not just that related to security. Kayla would be a stellar value add as an adviser and contributor of modified or original programming for any company he might be interested in investing in.

Once she calmed down, she'd see that.

Until then, he should probably make sure she got both "I'm sorry" éclairs *and* coffee from her favorite bistro in the morning.

He'd drop them off on his way to work. Maybe he should reorganize his morning so they could spend a couple of hours together.

They hadn't had off time together in a while.

It was just that spending time with her away from work came with temptations he had to fight. The uncontrollable passion they'd once shared had to be kept locked up tight. That kind of attraction didn't lead to anything good. It was exactly what had been his mother's downfall and the reason his father, whom even Andreas could acknowledge was generally an honest, if bullheaded man, had an illicit affair.

Keeping their past firmly in the past should have grown easier as the years progressed, but the opposite was true. Andreas found himself admiring Kayla in a very personal, very sexual way at the least convenient times.

But he could not allow his own weakness to damage

their friendship. He'd worked too hard to find a place in his life for her more permanent that bed partner.

Kayla turned on her phone as she stepped off the commercial flight into the tunnel leading to the JFK airport. One long beep indicated multiple text messages and another different tone told her she had at least one voice mail.

She looked for someplace to step out of the flow of busy foot traffic and spied an area set aside for business travelers to work. Making her way across the wide hallway, Kayla barely missed bumping into a woman pushing a stroller at a faster clip than Kayla usually jogged.

A man in sweats and sandals bumped into Kayla, knocking her right against a wall. She waved away his hurried apologies, more bothered by the idea of having to talk to a stranger than the sore spot on her shoulder from hitting the wall.

Kayla hated traveling alone and missed Andreas's commanding presence that always seemed to create an opening, no matter how many people crowded the walkways. The traitor.

Kayla's phone buzzed as she reached the relative safety of the business area. She grabbed it and was relieved to see Hawk Security. She'd emailed Sebastian Hawk the night before, but hadn't heard back and wasn't even sure he'd be able to work her into his schedule.

Kayla answered quickly. "Hello."

"Miss Jones?" a female voice asked.

"Yes, this is Kayla Jones."

"I'm calling for Sebastian Hawk."

Her gut clenched with both hope and trepidation. "Yes?"

After telling the secretary that Kayla was in New

York *now*, she learned Sebastian Hawk wasn't, but was expected back that night. And while he always spent his first day back from any business trip with his family, he could fit her in for a lunchtime meeting the day after.

"That would be great." She made no effort to curb the enthusiasm she felt from showing in her voice. She was grateful and she let it show. Her home was on the line and even if Sebastian Hawk didn't know it, Kayla did.

"If you'll give me your email address, I'll send you the calendar invite."

"Thank you." Kayla recited her particulars, thinking Sebastian Hawk's secretary might actually be as organized as Bradley.

Kayla ended the call and looked around the airport, wondering what she was going to do with two days of no work and for the first time in six years. Deciding to check her other messages, she discovered that Andreas had texted her multiple times. Bradley had texted her twice and there were three voice mails. At least one of those was from someone besides Bradley and Andreas.

Kayla listened to the voice mail from the project lead on the revamp of their school security software. Ten seconds into the message, she wasn't sure if she wanted to laugh or cry.

Not that Kayla cried anymore. Crying never changed anything and it gave her a headache.

Her project lead was calling on behalf of Bradley, who was basically begging her to save *his* sanity by calling Andreas.

Kayla shook her head, but she dialed Andreas's private number.

He picked up on the first ring. "Where the hell are

you?" His voice boomed across the line, laced with a heavy dose of worry.

"I *told* you I was taking the day off."

"You weren't home this morning when I stopped by."

"So? Maybe I spent the night in someone else's bed." She wasn't sure why she said it, but she didn't regret the words.

Dead silence met her words and Kayla even checked her phone to make sure the call hadn't dropped.

"Andreas?" she finally prompted.

"You don't sleep with strangers. Hell, you don't even talk to them."

"Casual sex doesn't require a long conversation."

"You would know this how?" he demanded.

"You sound like a jealous lover." And while they might have been lovers at one time, he'd never been jealous.

He'd been very careful to explain that while he expected monogamy, it wasn't because they were in a romantic relationship. It had been a matter of health safety.

"I sound like a concerned friend."

"I'm an adult."

"Who won't tell me where you are."

"You don't need to know my every move."

"You are being obstinate."

"I'm—" was all she could get out before Andreas interrupted her.

"What the hell are you doing in New York?"

"How do you know where I am?"

"I used the locator function on your phone." Which he hadn't been able to do while she'd had it off on the plane.

"I didn't give you the code so you could track me like an errant child."

"I did no such thing."

"What would you call it?"

"A concerned friend and business partner."

"Well, now you know where I am."

"But not why you are there."

"Why do you think, Andreas?"

"You're meeting with Hawk?"

"Yes."

"But he's out of country."

"Until tonight."

"You only took one day off."

"I'll be taking the rest of the week off."

"*What?* You can't do that!" The genuine shock in Andreas's voice was laughable.

The fact he was shouting would have alarmed her if she wasn't numb. "In fact, I can."

"You never have before."

"There's a first time for everything."

"What are you going to do with Hawk out of town?"

"Whatever I want. I'm taking a page out of your book."

"I don't take time off without notice."

"You're selling the company, that's the biggest abandonment I can think of."

"I'm not abandoning anything. Part of the purchase agreement between Hawk and myself is a guarantee of employment for the current employees, provided their performance continues to meet expectations."

"How nice."

"You didn't need to meet with him to confirm that," he said, sounding hurt.

"I'm not meeting with Hawk to make sure the other employees have jobs on the other side of this buyout."

"Then why are you meeting him?"

"To make plans for *my* future."

"I already have plans for your future!"

"How interesting, since you haven't brought any up to me."

"I did. I want you to go into business with me again."

"No."

"You don't mean that."

"I do." She'd never meant anything more.

He must have heard the conviction in her voice, because Andreas didn't come back with an instant rejoinder.

"You've made plans for your future and your bride pimp is so right. They are not my business, but *my* future and the plans I make for it are *mine*."

"She was wrong."

"Maybe you should have told *her* that and I would believe you."

"I do not lie."

"You just keep things from me. Important things."

"I told you, I was going to talk to you about it."

"If my opinion, much less my feelings, mattered, you would have talked to me before you talked to Sebastian Hawk." Before he hired Genevieve.

"Is that why you insist on meeting with him? Paying me back?"

"I'm not that petty. This is about my survival." As the words came out of her mouth, she realized how very true they were.

Andreas wouldn't understand. As hard as it had been to lose his mother, as much as he despised his father's hypocrisies, Andreas had never been without a home to call his own. He had not been a three-year-old little girl left in the bathroom of a truck stop. He didn't know what it was to have his entire world ripped out from under his feet, not once, but twice before reaching the age of eighteen.

If he did, he wouldn't be selling the company that gave Kayla her first sense of belonging and security since the death of the foster mother who had coaxed Kayla back to speech.

"I would not leave you without resources. Have I not proven that to you?"

"No. You've pretty much proved the opposite, Andreas." Pain coalesced in her throat, making it tight.

But she would not cry.

"No, Kayla...that is not what this is about."

"I have to go, Andreas."

"To do what?"

"Get a clue, Mr. Almighty Kostas. My life is none of your business anymore."

"Why? What is really going on here?"

"I'm dumping a relationship that is toxic to me."

"I am not toxic. I am your friend."

She couldn't take another word, not without losing it, and she hadn't lost control of her emotions in years.

"Goodbye, Andreas."

She ended the call before he could reply. Now she just had to check into a hotel. Then she was going to do something. She didn't know what, but her time of waiting for Andreas Kostas to wake up and realize they were meant to be each other's family was over.

They weren't even friends, no matter what she'd always thought. If they had been, she'd have known he planned to buy a wife.

Andreas heard that ominous beep that indicated Kayla had hung up on him again and shouted, "Bradley!"

His PA came rushing into the office. "Yes, boss?"

"Get me to New York right the hell now. Charter a jet, whatever it takes."

"On it." Bradley turned to go.

"Keep tracking Kayla's phone."

Bradley waved his hand in acknowledgment.

"And find out what hotel Kayla is staying at. Book me a room beside hers. I don't care if they have to move other guests. Make it happen." He heard his father's voice coming out of his mouth and for the first time in Andreas Kostas's life, realizing a similarity with Greek shipping tycoon Barnabas Georgas didn't bother him.

If it took acting like an arrogant bastard to handle this situation, then arrogant bastard he would become.

CHAPTER THREE

PUSHING HER SUNGLASSES up on her head, Kayla laid her driver's license down in front of the desk clerk at the hotel on Times Square she'd made reservations at before she'd left Portland. "I know it's not 3:00 p.m. yet, but I was hoping a room could be found for me."

She'd booked a single with no frills and didn't care what floor they put her on. Unlike Andreas, Kayla didn't care if she got concierge level with turndown service. She just wanted some time in her room to unwind away from other people. She fully intended to turn off her phone too. No interruptions between her and her thoughts.

And maybe even a nap. There was a first time for everything.

The desk clerk typed something, presumably Kayla's name, into the computer, then straightened her shoulders. "Oh, yes, Miss Jones. Your room is available immediately if you like."

"That's great." After her conversation with Andreas, she was feeling drained. The cross-continental flight hadn't helped either.

The young woman waved at the concierge and suddenly there was a bellhop there ready to take Kayla's bag.

"Oh, I can get that."

"Let me, Miss Jones, please," the smartly dressed man who looked more like an extra in a mob movie than a bellhop said.

Kayla shrugged. She wasn't sure what it was about her pale melon wrap skirt and gray tank under a dark melon hi-lo knit jacket that said "wealthy lady who needs help" to the bellhop. Her comfy travel sandals weren't even from the designer side of her closet, but Kayla wasn't going to argue about it.

She just hoped she had appropriate cash in her Michael Kors backpack for the tip.

When the bellhop used Kayla's key to access the upper floor of the hotel, she got an inkling that he wasn't taking her to the original room she'd booked herself. When they got off on the top floor, she was sure of it. The smell of roses when she entered a spacious sitting area of what was obviously a superluxurious two-bedroom suite had Kayla cursing Andreas's name.

The bastard. He'd had Bradley change her reservations. Of course he had. The Greek tycoon was a control freak of the highest magnitude. And he was on his way to New York. Of course he was. Obviously, he intended to stay in the beautifully decorated suite with Kayla.

Andreas wouldn't see any problem with that. He hadn't been carrying a torch for Kayla for six long, interminable years.

She shouldn't be surprised. She really shouldn't. This was just like something the overbearing Greek tycoon would do.

Only she was. *What* did he think he was doing?

He had meetings. Much more important than hers. And a bride to find. And a matchmaker to make happy. And Kayla's darn business to stay the heck out of!

That last was the most important.

She was here to establish the rest of her life without Andreas Kostas in it. Didn't he realize that?

Maybe he did.

Cold chills washed down her body.

Maybe he wasn't as ready to let go of their friendship as she was.

Well, he was going to have to get over that little problem. He'd had a total of eight years, two of which included amazing sex, to figure out that they could be something more. What had the idiot done, though? He'd gone and hired a matchmaker, that was what!

He'd decided to sell Kayla's home! Her one place she felt safe.

Well, she wasn't putting up with that. He could go off and get married and have all the business challenges he wanted. Kayla might even come to the wedding, but *they* were done. Done as business partners. Done as best friends.

Just done.

When the bellhop asked what room to place her bag in, Kayla waved at the one on the left. She didn't care. What did it matter? This room, no matter how swank, was no more sanctuary than her condo back in Portland. The only sanctuary she had was her office and lab back at KJ Software and she wasn't going to lose that.

Kayla grabbed her phone out of her bag and tossed it onto the table.

To heck with staying here and waiting for Andreas to show up. She was going out.

She looked down at herself. Right. First stop, the Garment District. Shopping cured a lot of frustration. At least it did when you had money, and ever since she'd started working for KJ Software, Kayla's bank account had never been empty like back in the days when she'd been alone in the world without the company.

She was in a small start-up designer's boutique, trying on a dress that hugged her curves in a way that would require another layer. Maybe a jacket? A long vest? But it was her signature color. The perfect shade of melon in a ruched silk that made Kayla's breasts look a cup size larger and her bottom look like it was padded.

She turned to get another angle from the three-way mirror when a sound of masculine appreciation came from her left.

"Very nice."

She spun to face a blond who looked vaguely familiar. "Thank you, but I think it needs a long vest."

"To hide that gorgeous body? I don't think so." Blue eyes tracked her with heated approval that managed to feel like a compliment and not something smarmy.

Still, she rolled her eyes. "Are you trying to pick me up?"

He laughed, the sound genuine and amused. "I haven't noticed anyone giving you the attention you deserve."

"You're saying you noticed I'm alone."

"Yes."

"A woman can shop alone."

"Could you please tell my sister that? She insists not."

A young woman who also looked familiar in that way people do who could be celebrity doppelgängers said, "You *like* shopping."

"In women's clothing boutiques?" the flirtatious man demanded.

The younger woman laughed. "Okay, maybe not so much. Anyway, Chantal is coming, so you're off the hook. BTW, that dress looks killer. You've got to buy it."

Kayla looked back at the mirror. She did like the dress. She nodded. "I think I will."

Mr. Blue Eyes gave her another appreciative look. "Wear it tonight when we go out."

"You are trying to pick me up!" Kayla laughed, not at all offended.

He was too charming and good-looking. Besides, his sister was there. Said sister exclaimed, "Oh, you've got to go out with him, everyone wants to be seen with Jacob."

"Why? Is he somebody famous?" Kayla joked.

Jacob put a hand to his heart and staggered back, like he'd taken a shot. "I'm hurt. You don't recognize me?"

"You look familiar. Does that make you feel better?"

His sister burst into gales of laughter. "Oh, this is fabulous. The one woman in New York who doesn't know who you are." She whipped out her phone. "Just wait until my followers hear about this."

Kayla frowned. "I'm starting to feel like I'm really missing something here."

"I'm the lead in…" He named a new and rising-in-popularity Broadway production. "And the brat doing the tweeting? She's my twin, but she's also a famous model. Just ask her."

The beautiful younger woman put her phone where Kayla could see the screen. "It's true. See? I have over a million Twitter followers."

"I'm a software designer. I don't get out much," Kayla muttered.

Both Jacob and his sister laughed, clearly more amused than offended.

"So, you'll let me show you my city?" Jacob asked persuasively.

His supermodel sister grinned and winked. "Oh, do

say yes. It's been an age since he's been out with any-one who wasn't a total sycophant."

She didn't want to go back to the hotel, where An-dreas would be soon. "Maybe I will."

"Maybe we can start our evening early." Jacob jumped onto Kayla's tentative agreement.

"I hate to break it to you, but I'm not done shopping."

"I make a great shopping buddy." He smiled engag-ingly. "Just ask my sister."

"He really does," said the woman, still very busy with her smartphone.

And that was how Kayla found herself spending the next several hours in the very pleasant company of a Broadway star. It was kind of amazing. Other than a couple of people asking for Jacob's autograph, people mostly left him alone. New Yorkers took his presence and even Kayla's with him in stride.

"Do you want to stop at your hotel and get ready to go out?" he asked solicitously later.

No, she really didn't, not and risk running into An-dreas. Kayla's backpack had everything she needed besides the clothes and shoes she'd bought while out shopping.

"It might make more sense to get ready at your place so you could get ready at the same time," she offered.

"I like the way you think."

He put the arm not carrying packages for her around her shoulder. "Don't take that as some kind of invita-tion."

"I wouldn't dream of it." The laughter in Jacob's voice mocked her.

But Kayla smiled anyway.

Jacob lived in an older, secure building, not far from the theater district. Jacob came out of the bedroom dressed in designer jeans that showed off his manly assets in delicious ways and a white silk shirt.

He approached Kayla, who had changed into the new dress in his tiny bathroom and applied makeup before pulling her tight curls into a messy bun on top of her head. Masculine approval glowed in his blue eyes. "You look amazing, Kayla."

"Thank you."

Jacob put his hands on her shoulders, intent unmistakable in his eyes.

Pounding on his door startled them both. Jacob jumped back. "What the hell?"

"Open the damn door," Andreas bellowed from the other side.

Kayla gasped. "Andreas."

More pounding. "I know you are in there, Kayla. Tarkent, open this door!"

Jacob's last name was Tarkent?

"Do you know who that is?" Jacob asked.

"My boss."

"Your *boss*?" Jacob asked. "Not your boyfriend."

"No. Boss."

"He sounds like a pissed-off lion."

The door shook with the force of Andreas's pounding. "Kayla!"

"Um, yeah."

"Do I open it or call the police?"

"I wouldn't call the police." She'd never seen Andreas in this mood. She didn't know what he was capable of, but she did know theater productions needed backers and backers meant money and Andreas knew how to manipulate money.

"Are you afraid of him?"

"Afraid of him?" Sudden fury filled Kayla and she

marched to the door. "The day I'm afraid of Andreas Kostas is the day I stop being Kayla Jones. I am not afraid of that man, or any other man, Jacob Tarkent."

She threw the locks and yanked the door open. Then stood there, her arms crossed, glaring at her boss, not moving one inch backward.

Andreas had to pull his hand back from another set of furious pounding. "There you are."

"Here I am. The question is, what the heck are you doing here, Andreas? I don't believe you were invited on this date."

"You can't go on a date with him. You don't know him!" Andreas looked as disheveled as Kayla had seen him in a very long time. His tie had been loosened to dangle away from his collar, the first button on his shirt undone. His hair looked like he'd been running his fingers through it, his face showing the signs that he'd missed his second shave of the day.

"I met his sister. I spent the day with him. I'm fine."

"You are not fine." Andreas managed to maneuver his way into the apartment. "You are coming back to the hotel with me and we are talking."

"I am going on a date with Jacob. Then if I want to I am spending the night with him. If I come back to the hotel, whenever that might be, you can explain to me how you found me *here*." She turned to face Andreas, bothered by the fact that he was now *inside* Jacob's apartment and that had not been Kayla's intention at all.

"He had to have set private investigators on you. They probably found you through my sister's tweets," Jacob said.

"Did you?" Kayla demanded, fury riding her like it hadn't in years.

Andreas's cheeks burnished red in admission of

guilt. "I am not leaving you here," he insisted stubbornly, without bothering to answer the accusation.

Jacob came up beside her, putting his arm around her shoulders possessively. "You are not invited on our date."

Andreas's jaw twitched.

Kayla wanted to feel something at having an attractive man's arm around her, some spark of desire and sexual appreciation. She didn't. She didn't even feel truly comfortable. If she wasn't so annoyed with Andreas and wanting to make a point, Kayla would have stepped away from Jacob's hold for her own sense of peace.

"Kayla, you and I need to talk." Andreas had that tone and expression he used when he was trying very hard to be reasonable but was a nanosecond away from losing his Greek temper.

"Not tonight," she denied.

"I canceled everything."

"Funny. I did the same thing. Only I'm on vacation time. Do you know what that means, Andreas?"

"No," he gritted out.

Andreas Kostas was a man who disliked not having all the answers. Who was she kidding? He hated not having just one answer out of a hundred questions. The man defined *overachieving perfectionist*.

"Oh, I know the answer to this one," Jacob drawled, not realizing what dangerous waters he was swimming into. "It means, Mr. Armani-Suited Businessman, she's not obliged to spend her off-hours with you. Talking or otherwise."

"Kayla is not merely my employee, she is my business partner."

Kayla snorted at that stretching of the reality of their situation.

"Am I lying?" Andreas demanded, his voice gone dangerously soft.

"Can I stop you from selling the company?" she demanded back.

Andreas's face went stiff, the color draining from his naturally olive complexion. "It is not uncommon for one partner to have controlling interest."

"Ninety-five percent is more than simple controlling interest." Her 5 percent still gave her leverage, though. With Sebastian Hawk, if not with Andreas.

"We built that company together."

"I used to believe that too. Until you decided *on your own* to sell it."

Jacob's arm fell from around her waist as he moved to stand between Kayla and Andreas. "As fascinating as all this business talk is, I get one night off per week and I plan to spend it showing Kayla the best side of my city."

"That is not going to happen." Andreas's tone had gone hard and icy.

Kayla could hear the warning in it if Jacob couldn't.

"That's not your decision to make," the Broadway actor said to prove his deafness.

Kayla almost groaned.

Andreas turned the full weight of his glacial green gaze on the other man for the first time since arriving at his apartment. "You would be smart to stay out of this."

"Are you threatening me?" Jacob asked, sounding unimpressed.

Andreas stepped forward so he towered over the other man. "My suit is bespoke, not Armani, and if you knew the difference, you might understand that I would be a very unpleasant enemy."

Kayla laid her hand on Jacob's arm before he could

reply. "Don't. He's right. He's talking about major money, Jacob."

"I don't care about his money, Kayla."

She smiled up at the actor, really liking the man, wishing again she felt even an inkling of sexual attraction to go with the liking, something that would make fighting Andreas worth it. But she wasn't putting Jacob's career at risk for principle alone.

"No, I know. You're a special guy. Good to your sister. Fun."

Andreas made a displeased sound.

Kayla ignored him. "I would have enjoyed tonight more than I think either of us could imagine."

"I'm an actor, I have a great imagination." Jacob's drawl was only slightly less suggestive than his wink.

She laughed. "I bet, but if I go with you, he's just going to follow us around. He'll figure out a way to ruin our evening." To ruin Jacob's career, or at least his current role.

"That sounds like pretty stalkerish behavior for a boss."

"He used to be my best friend."

"Until when?" Jacob asked, with surprising insight and compassion.

"Until yesterday morning when he told me he was selling our company out from under me."

Andreas made a sound that could have been hurt, but Kayla refused to look at him.

Jacob nodded. "I'm sorry."

"Thank you. For what it's worth, I was really looking forward to tonight."

"I don't think it was going to end like I was hoping, though." There was no accusation in Jacob's tone, just rueful disappointment.

She shrugged, but she couldn't lie. "Probably not."

"It would not," Andreas butted in with his obnoxious Greek hobnailed boots. "She doesn't do casual sex."

She rounded on him. "You are such an ass."

"And you are the best woman I know. Apprizing Jacob of the fact you are one of the best women he has had the honor of meeting is not a bad thing."

Kayla stared at Andreas, speechless.

Jacob burst out laughing. "You are one clueless bastard, aren't you?"

"I am a brilliant businessman." The bewildered offense in Andreas's tone was almost funny.

Jacob pulled Kayla to him and laid a screen-worthy lip-lock on her. "It really was a pleasure meeting you, Kayla Jones. If you can get away from your boss while you're in town, call and we'll do something."

She grinned. "I will."

Andreas glowered at Jacob the entire time Kayla collected her things, giving the actor one-word answers to his conversational forays, if the Greek deigned to answer at all.

Andreas put his hand out imperiously for her bags. "Let me help you."

"I'm fine."

He didn't bother to argue, just waited for her to pass the packages over. Andreas had an innate sense of courtesy that her own sense of independence had never been able to win against.

He somehow managed to get between her and Jacob so the other man could not kiss her again before they left either, all the while avoiding shaking the actor's hand in farewell because of the packages Andreas had taken from Kayla.

"You think you're a slick operator, don't you?" she demanded as they rode the elevator downward.

"I know what I want."

"Really? What part of what you want has you in New York right now, Andreas? Because I really don't understand. You want to sell the company? I can't stop you. You want the bride pimp to find you a wife? I'm pretty sure *that's* not going to happen while you're here. So, what purpose is you being here going to serve?"

"I'm here for you," he said, like it should be obvious.

"But why?"

He didn't answer. Not in the elevator, not when they walked out onto the crowded New York streets, not when they got into the cab he hailed. In fact, Andreas remained stubbornly mute until the cab stopped in front of their hotel, where instead of letting her out, he imperiously waved at the doorman.

The man came over and Andreas handed over Kayla's packages with instructions for taking them up to the suite along with a generous tip.

"Where are we going?" she asked when Andreas got back in the cab.

"You were going to dinner. I would not deprive you of nourishment."

"We could have ordered room service."

"You were looking forward to a night out on the town."

Was he kidding? "Not with you."

"We are still friends, Kayla."

"I'm not sure we are, Andreas." It hurt to say.

The tightening of his jaw said he didn't like hearing it either. "Do no say that."

"Don't pretend like it matters to you."

"Of course it matters!" he roared.

Kayla jumped, shocked. Andreas did no lose his temper. Not with her. Not like this.

"Six years ago, you told me how much I mattered to you. I was just too desperate to believe something else."

"What? What are you talking about six years ago?" He turned to face her in the back seat of the cab, green gazed laser-like focus entirely on Kayla. "I thought you were angry about the meeting yesterday."

Kayla could feel the tears at the back of her throat, burning in her eyes. "I did too, but it's all part of the same thing, isn't it? I've never been more than a means to an end to you. What I don't understand is why you're here, why you tracked me down to Jacob's apartment, why you had to ruin my night with him. I guess I've never really known you, have I? I never thought you were petty."

"Petty?" Andreas demanded in a near roar. "The only reason that damn playboy still has his coveted role on Broadway is because he tried to protect a woman I care about very much."

"You don't care about me. You have never cared about me." Of that one fact Kayla was absolutely certain.

She'd been the piece of the puzzle Andreas needed to get his business off the ground. The brain behind the software to make the dream a reality so he could thumb his nose at Barnabas Georgas and prove that Andreas Kostas didn't need his father's money or his name, or anything else from the family that had hurt him so much.

"Turn this cab around!" Andreas sounded as out of control as she'd ever heard him, his big body fairly vibrating with stress.

"What do you mean?" The cabbie's hand gestured

wildly. "I can't do no U-turn. This is a one-way street, buddy."

"Take us back to the hotel," Andreas demanded in only slightly lower decibels.

Kayla crossed her arms over her chest and glared. "I thought we were going out to dinner."

"We are not having this conversation in front of a room full of strangers."

"Sounds more like a fight from where I'm sitting," the cabbie piped in.

Andreas ignored him and shook his head at Kayla. "You don't understand."

"On that we agree."

He didn't look calmed by that acknowledgment. The silence between them on the ride back to the hotel seethed with resentment and things left unsaid.

Kayla was terrified that after tonight the only person she'd considered family wouldn't be anything but a bad memory. But if she was right, if her place in his life was what she thought it was, that was all he'd been for six years and she'd been fooling herself all along.

CHAPTER FOUR

ANDREAS HADN'T BEEN this out of control since his father had come storming into Andreas's life, demanding he move to Greece, forcing him to use the Georgas name, pretending it meant something that they were blood.

When it hadn't meant anything at all. He'd hated being a Georgas. Hated living in that mausoleum mansion that had been the family home for generations.

Formally recognized as heir to the Georgas shipping empire, Andreas had been trained to his father's likeness, all the while planning his escape.

He'd wanted nothing of the man who could so callously discard the woman who had loved him with her whole heart. Melia Kostas had been an amazing mother who had not allowed a broken heart or the rejection of her family to stop her from raising her son to believe he had value and that he was worth every sacrifice she'd had to make to give him a different life.

She'd immigrated to America, only to die when Andreas was a teen, leaving the door open for Barnabas, that bastard, to come swooping in. That was the one time in Andreas's life that he'd felt completely helpless. He'd done a lot of yelling before settling down to plan.

Not until today had he felt so completely at the whim of another again. He had not felt such fear since the day his father had him physically carried onto the Georgas private jet and forced to fly to Greece against his will. Kayla leaving Portland, *leaving Andreas*, had paralyzed him. They were a team. Didn't she realize that?

Clearly not.

Never was his temper so close to the surface, so beyond his control.

But seeing that playboy actor's lips on his Kayla's face? That had made Andreas see red. She deserved better.

Kayla Jones deserved the best.

Maybe once Andreas was settled down with a wife who would complete his revenge plan on his father, he would hire Genevieve to find Kayla her own Prince Charming. A man who would care for her like she deserved. Someone who could appreciate the rare gem that she was.

Not some damn New York actor just looking to add another beautiful notch to his bedpost.

Andreas shifted in his seat, trying to control his urge to demand Kayla explain her remark about *six years ago*. It wasn't just a restaurant full of strangers he didn't want witnessing their very private conversation.

Andreas had no intention of giving their nosy cabbie any more fodder for his curiosity.

When they arrived at the hotel, Andreas waited on the sidewalk for Kayla to scoot out of the back seat. He would usually go ahead of her, trusting her to follow, but in her current state, he wasn't taking anything for granted.

She stopped in front of him, tugging the hem of her sexy little dress down. It hugged every curve, reminding him of how beautiful she was, that no other woman had ever measured up to the perfection of Kayla Jones since that first day he'd seen her across the quad at university.

He shoved those thoughts away. "Are you ready to go inside?"

"Do I have a choice?" she asked, 100 percent attitude.

Rather than grab her, he shoved his hands into his pockets. "You act like I'm some kind of tyrant."

"Do I need to remind you of the events of the last hour?" she asked in that sarcastic tone that made him want to do things he'd made himself forget.

He forced an even tone. "None of which would have happened if you had been waiting in the suite when I arrived."

"That was not going to happen."

"So, you wanted to go shopping." It had not surprised him to find out she was in the garment district. Kayla liked to shop when she was stressed. She'd worked out a few knotty computer codes with "shopping therapy," as she called it. It was discovering she was with Jacob Tarkent that had Andreas's blood pressure spiking. "Did you have to pick up a date?"

Kayla stepped past him with a saucy sway of her sexy hips. "He picked me up."

"I figured." Andreas followed, forcing himself to ignore the way her dress and attitude were affecting his libido.

He had six years' experience ignoring these sexual urges. It shouldn't be so damn hard.

"So? I'm single. It's allowed."

"You are in a strange city. He could have been any-one."

"But he's not."

"No." As soon as he'd known whom she was with,

he'd had a background check run on Jacob Tarkent, by Hawk's company coincidentally.

They were very thorough and fast.

"So, you knew I was safe."

He put his hand on her arm, stopping them outside the doors to the hotel. "You didn't." And that was the damned point, even if she wanted to ignore it.

"I did." Oh, she sounded so sure.

"That's right, you think you can read people."

"I can. It's a skill you learn in foster care." Her feisty expression dared him to contradict her.

"It's not one hundred percent."

"Nothing is." She glared up at him, everything in her demeanor defying him, and that should not have been a turn-on. "Are we going to stand out here discussing this?"

"At least you are finally admitting we need to discuss things between us."

She rolled her eyes, her lovely latte skin flushed with anger. "I'm really annoyed with you, Andreas."

"I think you are understating the case." *Furious* seemed more like it.

Her gray eyes narrowed further. "Maybe."

"Definitely." That was okay. He was pretty pissed off himself. Not that he wanted to examine why. He just wanted to fix it. All of it.

They *were* friends. She was all he had left of family. Even if she didn't realize it.

"Let's go inside."

"Whatever you say, Commander."

"You are skating on thin ice."

"Oh, I'm shaking in my boots." Kayla did sarcasm better than anyone he'd ever met.

"You only ever say that when you aren't wearing any."

"The irony is all the stronger in that case."

He shook his head and took her arm again, needing to know she was with him. She didn't pull away from his hold, and the gratitude he felt was all out of proportion.

They rode in tense silence to the penthouse-suites floor. The old-fashioned apricot roses he'd had delivered earlier filled the sitting room with their heady fragrance. He'd noticed that Kayla hadn't bothered to read the card Andreas had included with the flowers.

He frowned. She'd also ignored the box of her favorite chocolates on the table.

A bottle of sweet champagne chilling in a standing ice bucket and a platter of fruit had been added to the offerings.

Kayla's gaze took all this in and then snapped back to him. "What is all of this?"

"I wanted you to be comfortable."

"With roses, champagne and chocolates?" she asked with clear disbelief.

"There's fruit too."

"Isn't that a little romantic for your employee?"

"You are my friend, my business partner, not simply an employee, and it's not about romance. It's about offering your favorites."

"Typical."

If by *typical* she meant he somehow screwed up and then made things better with an offering of food, then yes. It was typical. And usually, she allowed the gesture as the olive branch it was.

She gave a disdainful glance to the champagne.

"I'd rather have tea." Her tone said she wanted all her wits about her.

He'd thought he could use the advantage of alcohol, but then again, maybe he needed his wits about him too. He definitely didn't need alcohol lowering his sexual inhibitions around her.

"Do you want to call for it, or shall I?" he asked.

"I'm not sure I could eat right now."

She never ate when she was stressed.

"I'll munch on the fruit if I get hungry." His appetite, on the other hand, never got affected by emotions.

Emotions had no place in life at all.

She would be better off if she could push hers aside too, but then she wouldn't be Kayla.

She nodded and then crossed plush white carpet to order her tea. Once she'd done that, she headed to the bedroom her luggage had proclaimed to be hers. "I'm changing into something more comfortable for this talk."

"You look great."

"Yeah, well, I was dressed for a date. This is not a date. I'm changing."

He didn't know why the words offended or he felt the need to argue that point. Andreas clamped his jaw and refused to allow the words of denial to pass his lips.

If the woman wanted to change, let her.

Six years ago, it had taken him some time to overcome urges like this too. That was all it was, the reminder of the sexual relationship they used to have.

Nothing else.

They'd been lovers for two years. She'd been the most satisfying sexual partner of his life, but he'd realized she was something more important. She was a friend he didn't want to lose, so he looked for a role she could play in his life that would keep her in it. Because lovers didn't last.

He'd finally figured it out.

A business associate. He knew that meant they had to stop their sexual relationship, but the sacrifice would be worth it. By changing the nature of their relationship, he was guaranteed of keeping Kayla in his life long-term. Lovers came and went, but if she came into his budding company with him, she would be with him for the long haul.

It had worked too.

They'd been best friends ever since.

Only now she was saying they weren't friends anymore, because he was selling the company. Didn't she realize he had plans for both of them? Didn't she trust him at all?

She came out of the bedroom as a knock sounded on the door. Andreas went to answer it though it might have been natural to let her do so.

They were in a large city and though the hotel should be secure, he would not have her answering the door here.

He opened the door to the waiter carrying a tray with Kayla's tea things. Andreas directed the man to place them on the table before signing the ticket.

He waited for Kayla to fix her drink just the way she liked, with milk and an even teaspoon of sugar, before speaking again. "Explain what you meant about six years ago."

Her hand trembled as she picked up her cup, but she managed a sip. Then she looked at him, her beautiful gray eyes filled with pain and a determination that scared him.

Nothing scared Andreas anymore.

He was his own man.

No one could ever take that away again.

She pulled her knees to her chest, wrapped her arms around her legs. Classic Kayla self-protection pose. Even her sweats and hoodie were what he considered her armor.

Most women dressed up when they wanted to feel safe, but not Kayla. She dressed down, in sweats, a hoodie, thick socks. And as far as he knew, Andreas was the only person who knew that.

Her gray gaze regarded him somberly. "Six years ago you figured out a way to use me for your company."

"That's one way of looking at it."

"Is there another?" she asked, sounding like she thought she knew the answer.

"I found a way to keep you in my life longer than a lover would have lasted."

Her eyes widened, her expression mirroring shock and a little incredulousness.

"I liked you more than any woman I'd ever had in my bed. I had more tender feelings for you than anyone else, like I'd only ever allowed myself to feel toward my mother. I didn't want to lose you out of my life entirely."

"But as your lover I had a sell-by date that was fast approaching," she said, as if with dawning understanding and no small amount of horror.

It was true none of his other lovers had lasted as long as she had. "I didn't know how much longer we would be together as sexual partners, but I knew as business partners our relationship would last longer."

"And it did." She said this with a strange, very un-Kayla-like tone, like she was adjusting her thoughts, but not like the adjustment made her happy.

"It was a good move. We started working together,

became *friends*. Best friends. We're in each other's lives in a good way. A long-term way."

"Not anymore. You're selling the company. You're walking away." Kayla's voice was filled with such sadness, such finality.

It chilled Andreas right through. "I want you to walk with me."

"I'm not leaving KJ Software." There was no doubt there. No give. Absolutely no compromise.

It was like she'd written code with no *if...then* statement. In Kayla's mind, this was a closed loop of program.

"You don't mean that. There's so much more you could do. So many more puzzles you could solve." Didn't she realize? "You're brilliant. The whole world of computer programming is open to you. It doesn't have to be cybersecurity."

"I like the puzzles I solve now. That company is my home. I feel safe there."

Her home? It was just a company.

But looking at Kayla, for the first time, he realized they looked at KJ Software with completely different eyes. He might own 95 percent, but Kayla was invested in the company in a way he never would be.

Something cold opened up inside Andreas. It had never occurred to him that when all was said and done he would not be able to convince Kayla to move on to the next venture with him.

"No, your home is your condo." That *should* be true.

She shook her head, her expression repudiating his words before she ever spoke. "That's just where I sleep. Not where I feel safe."

"Don't I make you feel safe?" If he wasn't her safety, what was he to her? He wasn't just her boss.

She stared at him, something he couldn't read in her gray gaze. "You're getting married."

"That doesn't mean things between us have to change."

"Yes, it does."

"No. I say what happens in my life." He'd made that truth in his life since he'd left the Georgas family and Greece. She had to know that.

"You're making a new family. I won't be in it."

No. Those words weren't true. He wouldn't let them be true. "You are part of my life." Part of his family, but for some reason he couldn't say the words out loud.

"Maybe we still can be friends, but you can't be my safety. That wouldn't be fair to your new wife, to the children you'll have together. It's just not the way it works, Andreas. The company. It's all I have. I have to talk to Sebastian Hawk and make sure he's not going to take that away from me."

Realization hit Andreas hard. And it was one he did not like. Kayla needed security he, Andreas Kostas, could not give her. She felt threatened by the loss of the company and his marriage happening at the same time. Both were necessary for Andreas's final plan to prove to his father and the Georgas family that he did not need them in any shape or form.

Had never needed them. Would never need them.

The only way to give Kayla what she needed was to put off one or both of his stratagems and Andreas simply could not do that. He had worked too hard to make his plans a reality. Besides, he was finished with KJ Software. He'd been itching to move on to something bigger and better for the last year.

Kayla knew that, even if she was struggling with accepting it.

It had never occurred to him that she'd want to stay on. That the company itself had taken on a surrogate family role to her. That she considered it her stability factor.

"I wanted you to keep working with me," he told her baldly.

The look of utter sadness and acceptance in her expressive gray eyes said it all. "You want to keep building bigger and better businesses."

"Yes."

"Sometimes, businesses fail."

"Mine won't."

Her pretty lips tilted in a half smile. "You're so confident."

"You've called me arrogant a time or three in the past."

"Well, you are," she teased in the old way.

He shrugged.

"I'm not leaving the company with you."

She meant it. She really wanted to stay with the company and had every intention of doing so.

"That doesn't mean we can't be friends." Maybe they wouldn't work together, but they still lived in the same building.

She drank her tea and stared at him for a lot longer than he thought it should take to answer that statement, but finally she set her cup of tea down and nodded. "I guess you're right about that. Friendship isn't about always getting what you want. It's also about being there for the other person. And I suppose in your arrogant, pigheaded way, you need me."

"Enough with the name-calling."

"You broke up my date."

"I was worried about you."

"You could have been worried about me tomorrow."

"Stop pretending like you were going to have sex with him." The idea was an anathema.

"You don't know what I was going to do. You think you know me, but let's face it, Andreas, you thought I'd be okay with the bride pimp and I'm so not. You thought I'd be okay with selling the company and I still kind of want to shred your closet of suits over that one. You thought I'd want to leave KJ Software to start a new company and you couldn't have been more wrong about that. I'm not sure you know me very well at all."

He couldn't argue a single one of those sentences.

And something about six years ago had gone down very differently than he'd thought too, or it wouldn't have come up today. Andreas had the unpleasant sensation that she was right and that he did not know Kayla Jones nearly as well as he thought he did.

And if he didn't figure her out, he was going to lose the one person he still considered family.

That was not going to happen. Andreas Kostas had lost all the important people in his life he was going to let go of.

Kayla Jones was never going to be one of them.

Andreas finished answering emails, ignoring yet another text from Genevieve. He'd had no idea she was so demanding when he hired her. She'd acted very accommodating and happy to have him as a client. Her tenacity was well-meaning no doubt, but he had other things on his mind at the moment. Her in-depth questionnaire and business-mogul makeover were going to have to wait.

Why did he need to change his clothes and haircut anyway? He didn't have any trouble finding companionship dressing like a high-powered businessman. When he'd mentioned that to Genevieve, she'd replied he was looking for a wife, not a hookup.

He was still unconvinced.

He didn't want a wife who expected some laid-back guy who was going to spend every evening and weekend playing happy families. That wasn't Andreas.

Dismissing thoughts of his matchmaker, he replied to another text.

Satisfied with his morning's work, he was considering ordering breakfast and waking Kayla when the second bedroom door in the suite slammed open. She appeared, no wakeup knock necessary, her curls tied up in one of the scarves she wore to bed to keep them tamed. Its bright color at odds with the dark visage of her face. Her glare shot around the sitting room until it landed on him with the weight of a fully locked-and-loaded missile.

Gray eyes narrowing even further, she stomped toward him. Her body moved in ways his couldn't help taking an interest in, what with the way her peach satin sleep shorts and silky spaghetti-strap sleep top clung to her bouncing curves.

Damn it, he needed to remember that the passion they'd shared had been too consuming for good decisions.

She slammed her beloved smartphone down in front of him. "Fix it."

The phone beeped, indicating a text.

"Fix what?" They'd long ago established she was the more technically savvy of the two of them.

"That!"

The phone beeped again.

"What?"

She shoved it in his face.

His eyes focused on the screen. The text was from Genevieve. Demanding Kayla get Andreas on the next plane back to Portland.

"You gave your bride pimp my phone number."

"Yes." It had seemed like a good idea at the time.

"Call her right now and tell her to stop using it."

"Just ignore her texts."

"That's what you've been doing." Damn, Kayla's voice could register *pissed-off woman* when she wanted to, with a heavy dose of disapproval. "And her phone calls, I bet."

"She's not on this morning's agenda." And Genevieve needed to learn that Andreas dealt with things in his time, not someone else's.

Kayla's glare went nuclear. "Well, putting up with her harassment isn't on my agenda at all. Call her off, Andreas. Right now."

"You're in a bad mood this morning."

"I was woken out of a sound sleep by incessant calls and texts from someone I shouldn't have to speak to at all."

"I told you she wanted to talk to you."

"Andreas, I'm not kidding."

"You never sleep this late." Kayla was an early riser, like him.

"I wanted to sleep in. That's my prerogative. I'm on vacation." She looked at him like he was the one who was acting entirely out of character and suddenly not making sense.

Andreas didn't know what Kayla saw in his face, but whatever it was, she got that supremely annoyed, impatient "I've had it" look. He'd seen it very rarely, but when she got it, he knew things were about to go pear-shaped. He despised that look.

The one person in the world he actually minded being at odds with was Kayla Jones. "Listen, Kayla—"

She put up her hand, cutting him off. She didn't say anything, just made a production of turning off her phone and dropping it onto the table in front of him. Then she went back into her bedroom and slammed the door.

Since the day before she'd left her phone in the suite and gone off exploring New York alone, that didn't bode well. Andreas had been forced to resort to other means of tracking Kayla down. Means he preferred not to rely on today.

Not to mention, he did not like thinking of her being without a means of communication.

He picked up his own phone and dialed Genevieve's number.

"Finally," the woman exclaimed. "Andreas, you have to treat this endeavor with more respect than you have done so far."

"I did not give you Kayla's number in order for you to harass her. Do not use it again, for any reason. In fact, I want it deleted from your file immediately."

"Don't be ridiculous, Andreas. Clearly, contacting your assistant got your attention."

"She is not my assistant, she is the director in charge of research and development. Show her the respect she deserves."

"Be that as it may—"

"Delete the number."

"Excuse me?"

"I will not. Your behavior toward Miss Jones has been in every way rude and unforgivable."

"You left in the middle of your own bride search.

Matchmaking is a delicate and complicated process. It requires your full attention."

"No, it requires *your* full attention. That is why I paid you such a high retainer. I explained that I had a business emergency."

"Since your Director of R & D is there, can't she handle the emergency?"

"We are handling it together."

"I'm sure—"

"That you will take care of your business while I take care of mine."

"Part of my business requires your participation, Andreas. Had you forgotten the makeover? I suppose I could fly out there and do it in New York."

"No. There will not be time." Andreas didn't feel in the least guilty putting Genevieve off. "I will call you when I return to Portland."

"What about the questionnaire? Will you have some time for that?" she asked, trying to sound ingratiating, but only managing to be annoying.

"I will get to it when I can." Andreas allowed his growing irritation to leak through.

"I can't help feeling you're not as committed to this as you originally led me to believe."

"Genevieve, you will learn that I do not like being questioned." He allowed his displeasure at the continued questioning of the parameters he had already set to ice his voice over. "I will speak to you when I return to Oregon."

He set his phone down and noticed Kayla standing in the doorway to her room, her expression no longer all narrow-eyed anger. Andreas wasn't exactly sure what that particular look meant, however.

"Was that Genevieve?"

"Yes."

"Did you tell her to stop calling and texting me?"

"I told her to remove your number from her files."

"If I was home, I could take care of that myself."

He had no doubt Kayla could do exactly that. You didn't become a world-class designer of security software without being able to circumvent it. "You scare me sometimes."

"Nothing scares you."

Nothing he was going to admit to. "How easily you get into other people's computers and phones is going to get you into trouble."

"It's a natural by-product of designing the best security software." She stretched and yawned, her breasts pressing enticingly against the silk of her pajama top. "I'm going back to bed."

"What about breakfast?"

She shook her head at him, a barely there smile playing at the edge of her lips. "Nothing is stopping you from ordering."

"But you are going back to bed. How long will you sleep?"

"As long as I want, I'm on vacation."

"But if we are not at the pier in in an hour, we will miss the harbor cruise."

Kayla's generous lips thinned. "Harbor cruise."

"I thought you'd like to see a little of New York while we are here." She kept harping about being on vacation.

"Jacob was going to show me the city last night."

The unnecessary reminder set Andreas's teeth on edge. "He wanted to show you his bedroom."

"Maybe it had a great view."

Andreas stood up, suddenly too restless to sit.

"Maybe if you want some good views you should get in the shower and get dressed so we can make the harbor cruise."

"I never said I was going with you."

"Don't be stubborn for stubborn's sake."

She frowned. "I was going back to bed."

"You can sleep later. Right now, we have sights to see."

"No wonder you're not wearing a suit."

He'd put on slacks and a button-down shirt, no tie, no jacket. He was dressed down. For him.

"You still look like a power broker."

"I am a power broker." And it would do her little actor friend well to remember that.

Andreas Kostas might not recognize Barnabas Georgas as family, but there was no denying the bastard's blood ran through his veins, as did his ruthless nature.

Kayla sighed. "I didn't plan on staying here in the hotel with you."

"Where would you go?" Andreas demanded, not liking the sound of her plans at all.

Kayla got harebrained ideas in her head and sometimes she stuck with them. It had taken him three years to convince her to move into his condominium building and only after he persuaded the complex to offer her a unit at a significant discount that he secretly subsidized the purchase of. She could never find that out, or she'd move out of spite.

The woman had an independent streak a mile wide.

"A hotel without you in it."

"Am I really so abhorrent to you?" he asked, hurt in ways no other person would be able to cause.

Her mouth twisted and she stepped away from the

door, toward him, like she couldn't help herself. "Of course not. It's just…" She looked up at him, appeal in her big gray eyes. "This is hard for me, Andreas."

CHAPTER FIVE

"ME SELLING THE COMPANY?" Andreas asked.

"All of it." Kayla bit her lip, her body taut, her arms wrapped around herself, like she was protecting herself. "I feel like I'm losing you and the company all at once."

"You are not losing me."

She shook her head, her expression saying he just didn't get it.

"Kayla, you persist in seeing family in a way that neither you nor I have ever experienced." He frowned down at her, stepping closer to her to make his point. "In a way I do not intend to live. My wife will not supplant your place in my life."

"My place in your life. As your *friend*." She said the word like it left a bad taste in her mouth. *Was* his friendship something she preferred to leave behind?

That was not acceptable.

She belonged to him. Kayla was part of Andreas's life and she was not leaving it.

"Yes."

The distaste that flitted across her face was barely there, but he'd seen it.

"Damn it, Kayla, we've been friends since college, suddenly that relationship disgusts you?" he demanded.

"I didn't say that." She turned. "I'll get ready to go."

"We're not done talking."

"We are if we're going to make the harbor cruise." Her bottom shook in ways that gave him ideas he had no business thinking as she walked toward her en suite.

Memories assailed him and suddenly he wanted her like he hadn't allowed himself to in years. His dick pressed against his trousers, the urge to follow Kayla both so strong and so shocking, he almost gave in to it.

Damn it. It had been a while since he'd noticed Kayla the way he was noticing her now. What the hell was going on with him?

Whatever it was, he had better get it under control. Kayla had a place in his life and that place was not his bed.

Damn it. He needed Kayla to stop acting crazy so he could get his libido back under control once and for all.

Kayla wasn't sure why she'd agreed to go on the harbor cruise with Andreas, except she'd overheard him telling Genevieve to lose Kayla's number.

Just like she'd asked. And she'd realized just how important their relationship was to him. He'd left work, he'd left his big plans to find his perfect little wife. He'd left everything to chase Kayla down and when he found her, he'd stayed.

Was staying until she returned. She really didn't understand why.

It was as if Andreas was afraid that if he left without her, she wouldn't come back, and for some reason that mattered to him. A lot.

He'd had breakfast delivered when she came out, dressed in her teal skinny trousers, tan-and-white-striped tank and carrying a white knit jacket, which she would put on when they left. The only things in her signature color were her coral brushed leather flats and chunky necklace, but the slacks did great things for her thighs and bottom. It didn't hurt that the tank molded to her breasts just right without looking like she was trying too hard either.

The outfit would be wasted on Andreas.

"Do we have time for breakfast?" she asked as she walked into the sitting room.

Andreas looked up from reading the paper on his tablet. His green gaze flared with something that looked like lust, but that couldn't be right. "That is what you are wearing?"

"Yes."

"Don't you think it's a little...casual?" he finally asked after a significant pause.

"To play tourist on a harbor cruise?" she asked right back. "No."

Andreas frowned. "Are you trying to get picked up? Again?"

"What are you talking about?" Seriously. What was the man's problem?

"Your outfit. It's sexy. Last night, you were dressed like a woman ready to seduce. Is something going on here that I do not know about, Kayla?" Andreas did not look happy at the prospect.

"The only thing going on is that you are being an idiot, Andreas. This outfit is not sexy." Just attractive. Darn it. "So, it looks good on me. It's not a walking invitation for sex."

"From where I'm standing, it is."

"You're sitting and you're still being ridiculous."

"Don't be pedantic." He stood and pointed down to his obvious erection. "As I said."

"I'm not responsible for your...for you...for *that*."

"The point is, in fact, you are."

She didn't know how she felt about the hard-on in Andreas's pants. Clearly he wasn't happy she'd given him one. A few days ago, she might have been hopeful in this situation, but knowing what she now knew about his plans for the future, she realized any attraction he felt for her meant absolutely nothing. Less than nothing.

"That is your problem, Andreas. I've worn more revealing clothing than this in front of you. If you're that hard up, maybe you should spend the morning doing something other than sightseeing with me. I can call Jacob and see if he's still interested in spending time with me after how rudely I left him last night."

"You are not replacing me with Jacob." Andreas was suddenly looming over her, his body practically vibrating with the ferocity of his feeling.

Wow. Reaction, much? "Well, I'm not changing my clothes either." She glared up at him defiantly.

His hands fisted at his sides, his big body one large, muscled mass of tension. "Let's eat breakfast."

"So, we have time?"

"Yes," he gritted out.

"Good. I'm not always rational when I'm 'hangry.'"

He almost smiled at that. "I know."

They sat down to eat, the tension between them stretched taut. She couldn't help wondering if his not-so-little problem of an erection continued to persist and what it meant. Had he gone without sex that long? Was it a requirement of the matchmaker's?

From their past relationship, Kayla knew that Andreas was highly sexed. It had been a rare day they hadn't made love more than once, much less let a day go by without having sex. If Genevieve had Andreas on a no-sex diet while he auditioned wife candidates, then that would explain how he was desperate enough to get excited by Kayla.

She was careful to keep her distance while in the elevator later and in the car on the way to the harbor. Andreas gave her several brooding looks. He'd approved her jacket, but cursed in Greek when he followed her out of the top-floor suite and said something about the fit of her pants. She'd ignored him, but couldn't help smiling to herself, whatever the reason for the uncharacteristic attention.

When they arrived at the harbor, the line to get on the ship was long and Kayla told herself the cruise would be worth it. However, when they stepped out of the black luxury car, Andreas led her past the long, winding queue of people to a man in a white uniform. Andreas showed his identification and soon after they were shown their way onto the ship.

"VIP treatment?" Kayla asked.

"You know I do not like waiting in lines."

"I'm sure the people down on the dock do not either."

"We could have taken a private tour."

"I wouldn't have liked that."

"I knew that. For some strange reason, you like doing regular tourist-type things."

"So, you booked us on a public cruise, but arranged to board before the rest of the passengers."

"That about sums it up." Andreas led her to outside seats near the bulkhead. Kayla would be able to get as many pictures as she liked.

"You are a strange man."

"Says the woman who could live like a queen, but prefers to live like a peasant."

"Just a normal person. You've got a medieval streak a mile wide."

"Hardly."

"I choose to spend my money funding the shelter."

"And I have told you I would match your funds, but you turned me down."

"It was too much, and would have set back your plan to prove your worth to your family." Besides, Kayla for Kids was hers. In the beginning, she'd needed something that Andreas didn't have a part of. "Besides, I let you donate later."

Just not match her funds.

"I am not proving my worth to them." Offense laced every word of Andreas's reply.

Kayla just shook her head. "Then who are you trying to prove it to?"

"I know my own worth."

"I would have said so, yes, but this whole plan, it says otherwise." She'd never spoken so frankly to him, not about this, but she really had nothing left to lose.

Literally.

His plan was taking it all away.

Andreas stared at her like maybe she'd turned from Perl to Python programming language before his eyes. "My plan will show the Georgas clan once and for all that a Kostas does not need them to make his way in the world, that I am better than anything they could have ever made me into."

"Your father was a jerk, both when he rejected your pregnant mom with a payoff and when he came swooping in after her death to take you back to Greece, no matter what you wanted. But you've already proved you don't need him. You took back your mother's last name. You've made a life for yourself in America, not Greece. You made a success of KJ Software beyond anything they could have imagined. There's nothing left to prove."

"I will show them that I can make my own family without them."

And with those words, Kayla lost any hope that Andreas might not go through with his buy-a-bride plan. Genevieve was going to find him some ideal woman with a perfect pedigree, certainly not a mutt brought up in foster care because her own mother couldn't be bothered to raise her.

No wonder he'd dumped Kayla six years ago. Not only did he not love her, but she would never fit Andreas's vision for his life. She'd never even been in the running. Kayla would bet she wouldn't even make it past Genevieve's first screening process.

Not that Kayla cared.

She might not have all the credentials to be considered something special in Andreas's eyes, but she'd made something of herself too, despite her lousy childhood. And she was proud of that fact. It was why she was so committed to the shelter. She believed that given a chance, other kids could make good choices too.

Kayla felt the final death rattle in her heart for any chance at a future with Andreas and forced herself to look at the man next to her as the one thing he insisted on being. Her friend.

She dredged up the sincerest smile she could. "I wish you happiness with your future, Andreas."

"What just happened?" He searched her face as if trying to read her thoughts.

But Kayla pulled her emotions deep inside, where no one could hurt her, not even Andreas.

"Stop it, Kayla. Whatever is going on in your head." He grabbed her shoulders, his look intent, bordering on worried. "Damn it. Stop it, right now."

"Relax, Andreas." She pulled out the smile. The one that had always fooled the social workers. "Everything's fine. So, what are we going to see on this tour?"

"Don't give me that fake smile. Something just happened and I want to know what."

People started pouring onto the deck, filling the chairs around them, and even if Kayla had been inclined to answer Andreas, which she was not, there was no way it was happening now. He realized it too.

She gave a pointed look to his hands on her shoulders and he released her, his reluctance clear.

That look of frustrated endeavor on his face would have been humorous under any other circumstances. Some answers Andreas Kostas would just have to learn to tolerate going without.

They all had lessons to learn in life and he'd taught her one of the most painful.

Sometimes, you had to give up on dreams. Full stop.

Despite its tense beginnings, Kayla ended up enjoying the cruise very much. She snapped picture after picture on her smartphone as they approached the Statue of Liberty.

"You're going to run your battery out taking all those photos," Andreas teased.

She turned to him, unable to suppress a delighted grin. "Tell me this doesn't touch even that stone-cold heart of yours. Your mother immigrated to the US."

"Not via Ellis Island." But there was an expression on his face that said he was more moved than he wanted to acknowledge.

"Coming to America was a big deal for your mom, wasn't it?"

Andreas shrugged. "She had no life for her back in Greece. Her lover had paid her off, expecting her to get an abortion, something her faith would never allow her to do. Her entire family had rejected her."

"Because she was pregnant with you?"

"Because Barnabas Georgas was their livelihood and she was an embarrassment to him."

"That sucks." But Kayla knew firsthand that parents didn't always put their children's interests first.

Andreas gave a bark of a laugh. "That is succinctly put, Miss Jones."

She smiled, a blush warming her skin. She loved making this man laugh. It did not happen often.

Andreas's brilliant green gaze sizzled across her skin. "You are so beautiful when you do that."

"What?" she asked, feeling like somehow the oxygen had gone missing from the fresh sea air around them.

"Blush. It's lovely against your café au lait skin."

"That's a pretty way of saying *mutt*."

Andreas went rigid, his emerald eyes snapping with unexpected fire, his jaw hewn from granite. "What did you just call yourself?"

"I didn't call myself anything." She rolled her eyes. "Stop pretending you don't know what I mean. I'm not all pure Greek like you. My mom was some kind of mix of white whatever and my dad was clearly at least part black, or where did these lovely kinky curls come from?"

"That makes you typically American. Not a mutt." Oh, his voice was serious, each word pronounced with exaggerated care.

"Right. Whatever, Andreas."

His hand came up to cup the back of her neck, his other landed on her thigh, warm and heavy. "Not whatever, you will never use such a derogatory term in reference to yourself again."

"I bet it's exactly how Genevieve would describe me."

"If she ever made the mistake of doing so, not only would I fire her but I would make sure every business-man of my considerable acquaintance knew not to en-gage her services."

"Yikes, dial it back a notch, Andreas. She didn't say anything." Despite how the other woman clearly looked down on her.

"You are my friend, Kayla."

"The way you're holding me feels like more than friendship, Andreas." Kayla's heart was running way too fast, her breath coming in short little bursts.

If he didn't move away from her, she was going to make a fool of herself and do something spectacularly stupid. Like kiss him or something.

"It does, does it not?" Instead of moving away, he leaned closer.

The announcer said something about the statue and a flurry of photography went off around them, but Kayla could not make herself look away from Andreas. The expression in his eyes was one she'd seen many times before, but not for six years. She was afraid to trust her own eyes now. What if she was seeing what she had wanted to see for so long? What she'd absolutely given up on altogether not an hour past?

What if that look wasn't what she thought it was at all?

But she was no virginal teenager. She knew this feel-ing well.

The tension surrounding them had nothing to do with being right in front of the Statue of Liberty for the first time. It had everything to do with his lips being mere inches from hers, his torso being so close, she could feel the heat of his body.

"What will this feel like, I wonder?" he asked.

Then his lips covered hers before she could ask what he meant. And for the first time in six years, Kayla felt at home. Safe. Connected. Andreas's mouth moved against hers and Kayla kissed him back, shock giving way before the absolute rightness of the feeling of his lips against hers. Andreas kissed her deeply, his hand on the back of her neck holding her in her in place for his mouth to plunder hers, to stamp determined possession, the hand on her thigh moving up to her waist and around to her back until she was completely surrounded by her former lover.

The sound of clapping, wolf whistles and laughter finally broke them apart. Only then did Kayla realize what a spectacle they'd made of themselves and that the cruise boat was treading water in front of the statue for the tourists to take pictures. Many of whom were way more interested in her and Andreas.

The blush that burned her cheeks this time was hot and uncomfortable, prickling all over her body. Andreas, the jerk, just laughed, looking for all the world like he got caught kissing in public places like this all the time. Which she knew was not the case. Not even close.

She glared up at him. "Fix this."

"What do you want me to do?"

"Make them stop staring and saying those things."

"It is okay, Kayla. We were doing nothing wrong."

"We were kissing like a couple of teenagers."

"I'd forgotten how much I enjoy kissing you."

"I know."

"You sound annoyed by that fact."

"I'm not the one who decided we made better friends

than lovers. Oh, darn it." She looked around frantically, hoping no one had overheard what she'd just said.

No such hope. There were way too many people avidly interested in her and Andreas, hanging on their every word.

She bit her lip and stared up at him. "This is so embarrassing."

"Being my lover is embarrassing?" he asked, sounding offended.

She was going to beat him, she really was. "We aren't, not anymore." She wasn't saying that word again. Grown woman or not. Thank you very much.

His look was way too speculative for her liking, but all he said was "I think you'd better get your pictures if you plan to get any."

"You expect me to take pictures after that?" Her hands were shaking.

He smiled that brilliant smile he shared so rarely with others and pulled his own smartphone out, then proceeded to take several snaps of the statue, making sure she was in the foreground of a couple of them. He even did a selfie shot with them both. It was surreal and Kayla wasn't sure what was going on.

When the captain started the boat going forward again, Andreas put his arm around Kayla's shoulder like it was the most natural thing in the world. His thumb brushed up and down her neck, sending shivers along her nerve endings.

"What the heck are you doing, Andreas?" she asked, not even embarrassed when her voice went pitchy.

This? This deserved pitchy!

He kissed her temple and pointed at something on the shoreline. "Amazing, isn't it?"

"Where is all this affection coming from?" Kayla

started to wonder if she was in one of those dreams. The ones where you thought you were awake, but really you were still sleeping.

She'd never had one, but she'd heard of them.

"I like touching you. I had forgotten how much."

"Did you take seasickness pills or something this morning?"

His laughter was rich and warm and all hers. A sound he shared with so few people she couldn't help reveling in it, even if this was a superelaborate, really vivid, overly detailed dream.

"Or something."

She turned her head so their gazes met, knowing it was risky, but unable to have this conversation without eye contact. "What does that mean?"

"I've had a revelation." His grin was all straight, white teeth and positively blinding.

"What kind of revelation?" she asked suspiciously.

How could she be anything else? He looked like the kid who'd gotten the last cookie in the jar and knew where the others were hidden besides.

"I'll tell you when we return to our hotel. This is not a discussion we need to have in such a public place."

"Says the man who kissed me in front of an entire shipload of people."

"Only half the ship's passengers are on this deck."

"You're being facetious."

His smile was positively sinful and then he kissed her. Again. Not a passionate one, but certainly nothing platonic either.

Kayla gasped, floundering with feelings she'd barely held in check for years. Her mind fought with her heart and sadly her mind was not winning at the moment.

Still, she said, "You have to stop kissing me."

"The taste and feel of your lips says otherwise."

"Don't be a jerk."

"I assure you, I am not."

"Andreas!"

He squeezed her neck, like he was comforting her. "Do not worry, Kayla. It is all going to be all right. I promise."

"You can't promise that. Everything is messed up."

"Not anymore."

"How can you say that?" Nothing had changed. Except maybe he'd lost his mind. "I'm dreaming, right? That's what's happening here."

He kissed her again. Seriously. His lips against hers were firm and strong and possessive and real. Very real.

He broke the kiss only to kiss the corner of her lips like he always used to do. "There, does that feel like a dream?"

"I'm not answering that."

He made a pained sound. "I too have had dreams, but I have done my best to forget them in the morning."

"Andreas! There are children around." And avidly interested adults.

"As I said, a conversation for later."

"I'm not dreaming."

"No, Kay-love, you are not."

"I never understood why you used that endearment when you don't believe in that feeling." And he hadn't used it in six years. Now all of a sudden they'd had a mind-blowing kiss and he was using it again.

He shrugged. "It is just a word."

It wasn't to her, but maybe that *was* why he used it. *Love* was just a word to him, like *honey* or *sweet-heart*. It meant nothing more, but maybe it meant nothing less either and that was what she should be focused on. Something was happening here.

Something weird.

Something he wasn't going to discuss around others, which made her think it involved sex. Andreas wanted sex with her. Did she want sex with him? Knowing he planned to marry some paragon of perfection for a business mogul's wife somewhere down the road?

Kayla deliberately turned her focus back to the view outside the boat and listened to the history behind the bridge off in the distance. Its architectural significance wasn't enough to get her mind off the idea of sex with Andreas, but she tried.

What was she supposed to do?

Could she have a final hurrah with Andreas without breaking her own heart? He'd broken it once, six years ago, and she'd never mended. It was still too cracked to even consider falling for someone else.

Would giving in to him give her that illusive thing called *closure* or do her irreparable harm?

How hard would it be to turn him down? The warmth of his arm around her shoulder, the way her body responded to that simple touch told her extremely hard. Leaning toward impossible.

But did she have a choice?

Would she survive a night of casual sex with Andreas Kostas and watching him walk away after like nothing important had happened?

If six years ago had taught her anything, it had been that watching Andreas walk away after intimacy was more painful than losing any foster family. Because he *felt* like family. He felt like he was supposed to be hers. Only he wasn't. Not really. They were *friends*. And that was all Andreas would ever allow her to be.

For him that was clearly an important role. Important enough for him to drop everything to follow her and stay with her until she returned where he considered she belonged, but he didn't want the kind of belonging that she'd always craved. He didn't want to be her family.

"New York is a beautiful city. If it was not so full of people, I could live here, I think." Andreas's words broke into her musings.

She gathered her thoughts and pressed them back into the recesses of her mind and heart, where they had to stay, just like they had for six years. "It is. I never realized how beautiful. I think I'll always fit with Portland best, but I could visit New York again and stay longer."

"Perhaps we will."

She didn't reply. They'd traveled together before. Maybe they would again. Maybe his wife wouldn't care who traveled with the couple on their trips. Maybe Kayla would get to the point that seeing Andreas and his wife didn't rip through her insides with all the pain of a serrated knife.

Maybe never.

CHAPTER SIX

DESPITE THE AMAZING scenery and the fascinating narration, the rest of the cruise passed in a blur for Kayla.

Andreas never let up on his affectionate touching, eliciting a reaction in her body she did her best to ignore. Because the longer it went on, the more convinced she was that she had to tell him no.

No sex. No last night together before he moved on to marry someone else.

"Do you want lunch?" he asked as they were led to early disembarkation ahead of the other passengers.

She was about to answer in the negative when her stomach growled.

He smiled. "It seems you do."

"Let me guess. You've already got reservations."

"Naturally."

There was no car waiting for them, but a pedicab driver stepped forward. "Mr. Kostas?"

Andreas nodded.

"This way." The man indicated a newer cab with red leather seats and a motorized bicycle attached.

"We're taking a pedicab?" Kayla asked.

"I thought you would enjoy the experience." Andreas handed her up into the cab, for all the world like they were on a date.

Not that he ever treated her with a lack of courtesy, but things were feeling distinctly personal and guy-girl in the guy-expecting-sex-at-the-end-of-the-date kind of way.

The pedicab driver started peddling, weaving in and out of traffic in a truly alarming way.

Kayla gasped at a close call and Andreas took her hand. "It is all right, *pethi mou.*"

"Greek endearments? Really?" He was pulling out all the stops.

Andreas laced their fingers. "This is one of the company's best drivers. I made sure of it."

"I have been driving cab here for two years," the man said with a slight Eastern European accent.

Kayla asked about it and learned he was from a small village in Russia. He had his engineering degree, but had to take more schooling to qualify for the jobs he wanted here in the States.

Kayla was fascinated and asked more questions until Andreas interrupted, clearly annoyed. "I believe you know enough of his life story."

"I do not mind your lady's interest, Mr. Kostas."

But for some reason Andreas did. It was almost as if he was jealous, which Kayla knew was ludicrous. He was not the jealous type.

"We should be at the restaurant soon," Andreas said to her, ignoring the cabbie's comment.

Kayla frowned. "Don't be rude, Andreas. That is not like you."

Which was not strictly true. He could actually be really rude when he wanted, but he tended not to be impolite to people in a position like the cabbie's. Andreas didn't throw his weight around with what his family might consider the servant class. He'd seen enough of that living in Greece, he'd confided to her once.

"I will tip him extra if that will make you happy," Andreas replied grumpily.

She frowned. "You are being crass."

"Nothing I say will please you, but you hang on his every word." Oh, her ex-lover sounded seriously annoyed.

"I already know your history," she tried to explain.

"So, now I bore you?"

Oh, man. He was determined to take offense, wasn't he? "That is not what I said."

The cabbie coughed in a way that sounded suspiciously like he was covering a laugh.

Andreas gave him a suspicious look and Kayla knew things were going to go downhill fast if she didn't do something.

"What restaurant are we going to?" she asked with desperate enthusiasm. "Is it another tourist attraction?"

"Not exactly." Andreas turned his attention full on her.

She smiled up at him.

"I know when you're faking your smiles, you know that, right?" he asked with a clear frown.

She rolled her eyes. "Give me points for trying and tell me about the restaurant."

"I want your smiles to be real when they are pointed in my direction."

"I cannot guarantee that."

"That is not acceptable to me."

"Get over it."

"I will not get over it. You will stop giving me those fake smiles, Kayla. Save them for other people."

"Andreas, you are not being reasonable."

"I am eminently reasonable."

She laughed. Loudly. She could not help herself. "I'm sure that's exactly what Jacob thinks."

"Jacob has no place in this discussion."

"You do not get to tell me to just forget about someone like he never existed."

"Watch me."

"Watch me ignore you."

This time the cabbie's coughing could not hide his laughter.

Andreas glared at the hapless man and Kayla had never been as happy to arrive at her destination. The pedicab came to a stop in front of one of New York's many tall buildings, the walls seemingly made of glass.

"You will love the view at this place. Men, they take their women here to impress them," the cabbie said to her as he turned around to them.

Andreas grunted. It could have been agreement. It could have been *Mind your own business*.

"I'm sure you are right. Andreas is very good at guessing what I'll like." Except when it came to selling their company and uprooting her one certain sense of security.

The restaurant turned out to be on an upper floor with a view every bit as amazing as the cabbie had implied. Designed with the feel of Asian-modern fusion, the waitstaff were all dressed in crisp black and white and offered the kind of service found in only the most elite dining rooms.

They were perfectly solicitous, making sure she and Andreas had everything they needed. Kayla got the feeling that if they'd asked for something completely outside the restaurant's purview, the smart maître d' would have made it happen. The food was fantastic.

Andreas did his best to be an entertaining companion and that was doing nothing for Kayla's determination to tell him *no* about the sex thing.

At one point she glared at him. "Would you just stop?"

"Stop what?"

"Being so nice."

"You do not want me to be nice to you?" His brilliant green eyes widened with disbelief.

"No." She let out a huff of frustration when his whole body got into the incredulity thing. "I know what you want and the answer is no."

"Do not be so sure on either count, *pethi mou*."

"Stop with the Greek endearments too. They aren't going to work."

"Work at what precisely?" he teased, his eyes glinting with devilment.

She humphed at him. "*Whatever* your plans are for later."

"I assure you, you will like my plans."

"You always think that. You are not always right." The past forty-eight hours should attest to that definitively.

"I am *almost* always right." The humor was there in his voice, right under the surface.

"You're laughing at me."

"Maybe a little. Relax, Kayla. You are perfectly safe in this nice restaurant."

"It is a nice place. Very nice. It's a date kind of place, or the kind of place you take a client you want to impress. I'm neither." Both of them needed the reminder. "I'm not even sure how you got reservations on such short notice."

"Maybe you are simply a woman I care about, whom I would also like to impress, hmm?" he said, ignoring her comment about the reservations.

But that was a real thing, so he had to have exerted some kind of influence to get them. It made her feel more special than she wanted to. "Right. The day you care about impressing me, I'm going to eat my straw walking hat for breakfast *with hot sauce*."

"I hope you like hot sauce because I have always cared about impressing you."

"Don't be dumb, of course you don't."

"You are the only living person I do."

"That's... I..." She just didn't believe it.

"You know I do not care if I impress my Greek family."

"And yet you have this elaborate plan designed to prove to them how great you are."

"Or rather how much I do not need them." He said it like she should know this. She supposed he'd said it often enough.

She shrugged. She simply didn't believe him.

He raised his brows. "Who else do I care to impress?"

"Your future wife? Genevieve? Other billionaires? I don't know."

"None of the above."

"Then why would you care what I think?"

"Because you are my friend."

"You say that like you don't have any others and we both know that isn't true." Well, sort of. He wasn't a social guy.

Andreas Kostas was focused on his goals.

"Acquaintances, contacts, even casual friends maybe," he listed. "But not people whose opinions will ever matter to me enough to change the course of my life."

"Mine doesn't either."

He looked around them, then at her, his expression belying her words. "And yet here I am, in New York, when I am supposed to be in Portland having a make-over with the matchmaker."

"I wonder if she's going to give you hair extensions and a man bun. They're pretty popular right now."

Andreas shuddered. "Not going to happen."

"Oh, I know, she'll put you in jeans every day and those graphic tees that cling to your muscles and show off all the goodies."

"You like to tease me."

"Well, she's not going to leave you in your perfectly tailored bespoke suits and an overpriced businessman's haircut."

"Why not?" Andreas demanded, aggrieved.

"How should I know? You're the one who said she insisted on a makeover." Kayla thought he was plenty devastating just the way he was.

"Genevieve believes I am not approachable enough for husband material."

"What kind of husband does she think you need to be?"

"That is a good question and perhaps one I should have asked before paying her a twenty-five-thousand-dollar retainer."

"You think?" Kayla asked with heavy sarcasm.

Andreas frowned at her. "It is not as if I asked her nothing."

"Oh, I'm sure." Kayla started ticking off on her fingers. "Can you find me a bride who will fit these requirements? Will she be an asset to my business? She must be of a certain age and come from an acceptable background."

"You know I am not seeking to marry some wealthy socialite."

"That's not what I meant by *acceptable background*. I know you well enough to know your list of background attributes ran more to the lines of came from a stable home so she knows what good parenting looks like for when you have children." Which left Kayla out of the running right there. "Has an education, but isn't a PhD because you're enough of a chauvinist it would bother you if your wife was more educated than you."

"It doesn't bother me that you are smarter than me."

"I'm smarter at computers, not more intelligent and we have the same number of years in our degrees. Do not tell me if I had a PhD in engineering it wouldn't bother you."

"I would be proud of you. Do you wish to go back to school?"

Sometimes Kayla did. She loved learning, but more because she thought maybe someday she'd like to teach at the adult level. She didn't say that now, though. She just stared at him.

"What?" he demanded.

"My future plans aren't your concern."

"I do not agree."

"Andreas, you're going to be way too busy with your new venture capital firm to worry about what I do on the daily with my life."

"That is not true."

"You're so stubborn."

He laughed. "Have you met yourself?"

"Seriously, Andreas. You have this picture of how everything is going to be and you assume everyone is going to fall into it. That's not the way the world always works."

"As you have proven. We are in New York."

"So you have reminded me."

"It is a fascinating city, but I had no plans to visit this week."

"Neither did I before you dropped your bomb."

"It was not my intention to explode your life."

"Just move yours forward. I know."

"In my defense, I believed I was moving both our lives forward."

"Because you are arrogant and believe you know what is best for other people."

"Are you trying to pick a fight with me?"

"No. Just not letting you get away with anything. It's what I do."

"It has been too long since we shared a meal like this."

"You've been busy the past couple of months." She looked at him as the pieces started to fall into place. "Getting ready for the sale to Sebastian Hawk, right?"

Andreas grimaced. "You make it sound like I was sneaking around. I did nothing in secret."

"Then why didn't I know about it?"

"Because neither did I advertise the fact."

Kayla just shook her head. "Sneaky."

"No." His phone buzzed, indicating a text message of low priority, but then it chimed with Bradley's tone and Andreas looked at the screen, his face taking on a thunderous appearance as he read.

"What's the matter?" Kayla asked.

He looked up at her, his jaw set. "I'll explain in a moment." Then he dialed a number on his phone.

The sound of a woman's tones answering could be heard. If Kayla wasn't mistaken it was Genevieve.

Andreas barely listened for a second before saying, "You are fired."

Outraged squawks followed.

"I do not care what you saw on some social feed. I do not answer to you for my time and I will not have my instructions ignored or questioned by those who work for me. I expect a breach-of-contract portion refund of my retainer. Our business dealings are at an end."

The woman was no longer yelling, clearly trying to cajole Andreas into changing his mind, but Kayla could have told her it was a waste of her breath. He had made up his mind before making the call. Whatever she'd done had pissed him off on a level that there was no coming back from.

Not in Andreas's world.

"Goodbye, Genevieve." He ended the call without any more words.

Kayla stared at him. "What was that all about?"

Andreas looked pained. "You sure you want to know?"

With that look on his face? "Definitely."

"Genevieve wanted to come to New York to give me the infamous makeover, but I told her no. She decided this morning to ignore my wishes and come anyway. Bradley learned of her plans because my administrative assistant has ears everywhere and gave me a heads-up. Not that Genevieve hadn't told me herself in a text." Oh, Andreas sounded pissed.

"What would make her think that would be okay with you?"

"More like what made her think she might be losing a lucrative client?"

Kayla had a bad feeling. "And what was that?"

"Someone posted a picture of us kissing to one of those social media sites."

"But how would she have seen that? Surely they didn't know our names."

"A stroke of bad luck, I think. First an enterprising social media paparazzo saw you with Jacob and made it her mission to find out who you were, which wasn't hard after his sister apparently dissed you on Twitter for bailing on your date with him. The social media paparazzo happened to be on the cruise with us this morning. She decided to update the *scandal* of your botched date with Jacob by posting the picture of you and me kissing this morning."

"That's impossible."

"Improbable. Ridiculous timing. But not impossible."

"And Genevieve found out already?"

"She's a shark and stuff like this is blood in the water to her."

"Wow."

"That is no excuse for her ignoring my instructions."

"She was clearly worried about your commitment to finding a wife."

"I'm not married yet. I'm not even dating any of her candidates."

"Still."

"Still nothing. I fired her and she'll refund at least eighty percent of that retainer or she'll learn why there are risks involved targeting my demographic as her clientele."

"Okay, relax, Andreas. She told you all that just now?"

"She wanted me to know what a bad risk you are for involvement."

"That wasn't very nice of her." Not that Kayla expected any different.

"She's not a very nice person, but she is efficient."

"That's good I guess."

"Don't sound so enthusiastic."

"You're the one who fired her."

"You know I don't tolerate being ignored."

"I ignore you, you've never fired me."

"You are the exception to the rule." He winked at her and was too darn sexy with it. "Don't let that get out."

"We can't have anyone thinking you are a pushover." Kayla couldn't help the warmth that filled her at this reminder of her unique place in Andreas's life.

"Because I am not."

"No, you are not." He was selling the company out from under her after all. Andreas was no sentimental pushover.

"Have you finished?" Andreas asked, indicating her mostly eaten plate that she hadn't touched in over ten minutes.

"Yes."

"Are you ready to do some more sightseeing?"

Funnily enough, she'd expected him to ask to go back to the hotel. The sexual tension in the air was thick enough it should be an opaque cloud around them, but it was as if he was intent on building the anticipation to maximum levels.

He used to do that, back in the day, when they'd been lovers.

It had driven her crazy, in the best possible way.

A new-model, dark sedan was waiting for them when they reached the street.

"Where to now?" she asked as he handed her into the back seat, her slacks sliding easily over the plush leather seats.

There was something odd in his expression, almost hesitant as he joined her. "I thought the Brooklyn Bridge. You were fascinated by it this morning on the tour."

"It's beautiful."

"And you like bridges."

Portland had its own fair share, and she'd spent enough time exploring them, photographing them, walking across the ones with pedestrian ways and lost in contemplation staring at the river from their heights.

She shrugged. "They're like code, you know. They make a way between where you are and where you want to be."

"Your mind is unique, Kay-love. You realize this?" His voice was warm with approval.

And she wasn't sure what to do with that. "I know I don't think like normal people."

"What is normal?" His dark Greek brow creased. "Are we supposed to strive for average? I do not think so."

"Your arrogance is showing again." But she knew he absolutely believed what he said.

Andreas Kostas had never strived to be like other people. He'd forged his own path and taken Kayla down it with him.

He reached out and took her hand, his fingers warm and strong as they curled around hers, giving her a sense of reassurance and other feelings she did not want to examine right then.

It was too dangerous for her equilibrium.

His emerald gaze locked hers in place. "If honesty is arrogance, so be it, but you should never think less of yourself because you do not fit the mold of *normal*."

"You've gotten very affectionate all of a sudden." Not to mention complimentary.

Color slashed his masculine cheekbones.

"What?" she demanded.

He shook his head. "It is nothing."

But it was clearly something.

"You're losing your contractions again." It was a funny quirk of his, when he was really worked up. She wasn't sure if it was a speech pattern he'd gotten from his mother or something he'd picked up in Greece, but Kayla had always found it endearing.

"Do you think the way I dress makes me unapproachable?" he asked, apropos of nothing.

"Are you serious right now? Where did that come from?"

Andreas's lips gave a sardonic twist. "You know."

"Genevieve." The shark matchmaker.

"Yes. You know she wanted to make me over."

"Are you worried whatever matchmaker you hire to replace her will want the same thing?"

"There will be no replacement matchmaker."

Kayla wasn't sure how he was going to achieve his whole wife and two-point-five children with the white picket fence and billion-dollar bank account to rub into his father's face that way, but she couldn't deny a profound sense of relief.

"So, why ask?" Was he planning to go about this the old-fashioned way and date? Horror rolled over her. Did Andreas think Kayla wanted to be his advice buddy on this adventure?

"Why not answer?" Andreas pushed.

"I like the way you dress, whether it's in your bespoke suits or the blue jeans you keep hidden in your bottom drawer. You're just you, okay? If a woman needs you to dress like someone else to find you appealing, maybe she's not the right fit for you long-term, what do *you* think, Andreas?" If she sounded slightly waspish, well, life went on. Seriously, the man needed to catch a clue.

Maybe she'd buy him a fishing pole.

And some bait.

Rather than looking offended by her blunt speech, Andreas looked entirely too pleased with Kayla's answer. "I agree."

Then, keeping with his whole today-let's-shock-the-bananas-out-of-Kayla theme, he reached right out and ran his fingertip along the scooped neckline of her tank top. She gasped as his touch left all too familiar, if almost forgotten, static shocks of pleasure in its wake.

He smiled. "I like the way you dress as well, Kay-love. I always have."

"That's not what you said this morning. You were pretty critical of this outfit then."

"My perspective has changed since."

Five alarm bells went off inside her. How much more confirmation did she need? Andreas was in seduction mode. Full stop.

His eyes roamed over her, sending more tingles through her, touching her as intimately and surely as his fingertip had done. "I'd really like it if you wore the dress you had on last for me again."

"I wasn't wearing it for you." Her words came out far too softly, her breath coming in pants.

She needed to be firm, to let him know seduction wasn't an option, but her body was already softening for him, her brain throwing up all sorts of reasons why it was okay.

His eyes darkened, his mouth twisting with displeasure. "I know."

"You're too possessive for friendship, Andreas." He had to realize that.

"Am I?" He leaned forward until his mouth hovered right over hers, his lips brushing hers as he spoke again. "It doesn't feel like it to me."

She had no opportunity to answer as he kissed her. She tried to tell herself this was a very bad idea, but her lips were already responding to his, her body leaning into his heat, her mouth parting just slightly.

She would pull away and tell him *no more kisses*, in a minute.

But not yet.

She couldn't give up this feeling. It was too right. It always had been.

A sexual high like no other, but it was so much more than that when she and Andreas Kostas came together. It was a sense of belonging. It was home. It was family.

And for a woman who had none, that was addictive. Necessary.

And very, very dangerous.

Because she knew it wasn't the same for him.

For Andreas Kostas, it was all endorphins, satiation and stress relief.

His arms came around her, his hands pressing into her back, pulling her toward him, despite the restrictions of their seat belts. Someone made a mewling sound of frustration and she realized it was her. She wanted to be closer, no clothes in the way, much less seat belts.

She might have been embarrassed if there was room in the maelstrom of emotions inside her for such a thing. If he wasn't making his own masculine sounds that said he wanted the same thing.

The realization of how far they both wanted to take what should have been a simple kiss should have shocked her back to sanity, but she was sinking into the crazy too fast. His lips were too good, too right against her own, sending messages along nerve endings so her whole body was totally on board with the insanity. His tongue pressed oh, so perfectly into her mouth, so sexy, so enthralling.

Her thighs pressed together, heat pooling in her core, an ache building inside her that she knew could be assuaged only one way. One of his hands slid down her back, then along her waist and up her rib cage before cupping the bottom of her breast.

She moaned. Gripping his shirt with both hands, her fingers curled tight, unable to let go.

The kiss turned full-on incendiary, both of them biting and licking at one another's lips.

Kayla's moans mixed with his deep, masculine noises, more like growls than anything. She would be straddling him if she wasn't tethered by seat restraint.

Something about that made it even hotter.

The fact she couldn't do what she wanted, and, oh, how she wanted.

He pinched the hard tip of her breast through her top and lacy bra, sending shock waves of delight through her. She'd always had really sensitive nipples, but only Andreas had known what to do with that truth.

Or *how much* to do with it.

Now both his hands were on her, manipulating her fleshy curves, pinching and rolling her nubs, the two layers of cloth no impediment to sensation, Andreas expertly using the silky texture of her bra against her nipples for maximum stimulation. His kiss continued to push her passion higher and higher, everything inside her spiraling out of control. It had been so long since she'd felt this level of desire, wasn't sure she'd *ever* known anything this strong.

Even with him.

There was something to be said for giving in to a sexual need that had grown over years rather than days, with someone she'd known as long as she'd known Andreas, the one person in the world she trusted as much as she did him. On a level she could never trust another.

Despite his actions of the past forty-eight hours.

Kayla let herself go, knowing deep inside, where it really mattered, that she could trust Andreas to catch her.

And her body spiraled completely out of control, an incandescence of pleasure building, her womb spasming, her thighs clenching even tighter as the heat and need grew there.

He kissed along to her neck, giving her love bites and whispering seductively in her ear. "Are you going to give me your pleasure, *pethi mou*?"

She shuddered as his words registered on a very visceral level.

"That's right, Kay-love. Your passion is so beautiful." He nipped at her earlobe. "And it is mine."

"Andreas."

"That is right. It is me, no one else." He breathed gently into her ear.

She shivered, chills of sensation skating along her already overloaded nerves. "Possessive."

"Yes." Then he was kissing her again, his mouth claiming hers with unmistakable intent, his hands busy on her body, touching her so skillfully, drawing out the pleasure.

He nipped at her bottom lip at the same time as he squeezed both her hard nipples with exquisite pressure.

And that was all it took, her climax washed over her, at once familiar and all new at the same time, drowning her with ecstasy. With a final tweak to her sensitized flesh, he moved his arms back around her, giving Kayla a sense of safety and warmth as the gale-force winds of sexual satisfaction buffeted her.

CHAPTER SEVEN

HE BROKE THE KISS, nuzzling against the apex of her neck and shoulder again, inhaling as if taking in the very essence of her through her scent. "That is right, *pethi mou*, show me how perfectly we fit."

She let her head fall against his, her face warm, her body suffused with heat and a wholly inappropriate sense of well-being. "You are very bad for my self-control, Andreas."

"You said I was suddenly affectionate." His words sounded like secrets whispered quietly in the back of the luxury car.

"Yes."

"I could not touch you and maintain the friendship line." It sounded like a painful admission.

And yet… "No, that can't be right." He'd dismissed her from his bed so easily.

"I promise you."

Confusion filled her. Andreas did not lie. Not to get what he wanted, not to seduce. Not to convince. And his promises? He never broke them. There was also no denying the evidence as she managed to let go of his shirt, one of her hands brushing a rock-hard erection as it dropped into his lap.

"You are still needing."

"It can wait."

Oh, how many times had he said that very thing six years ago? He turned self-denial into a fine art and the springboard for her ecstasy as well as his own ultimate and very loud, energetic satisfaction. Andreas was apex sexual alpha.

Primal man.

"You are winding me up," she accused with little heat.

His smile was too damn sexy. "Only in the best way."

A tap on the door window alerted her that they were at their destination. She had no idea how many minutes the car had been stopped.

Kayla groaned. "How long has he been standing out there?"

Andreas shrugged.

She pulled away and looked around her. The privacy darkening shield was closed between the chauffeur and the back, the tinted windows preventing any curious New Yorkers from witnessing her and Andreas's heavy make-out session.

"I can't believe we just did that." Only, really, she could.

Andreas lifted one brow. "It was inevitable."

"Because I dressed too sexily today, according to you?" she demanded, not liking that excuse.

He shook his head. "Because from the moment I thought I might lose you, the need to reclaim you in a very primal way has been paramount."

There was that word again. "You just admitted to being more Neanderthal than modern man."

"Did I?" He asked, sounding more amused than offended.

"I'm pretty sure."

"Maybe I'm just more Greek than either of us ever realized."

"Or, you know, just a throwback."

"You enjoyed it."

"The driver is waiting," she reminded him, instead of answering.

His very predatory smile said he knew the truth. And really, after climaxing from, well...making out, what could she have said? *No, I didn't?* Kayla didn't lie.

Not outright.

Omission? That was something else entirely. She'd never told him she loved him and she never would. It would be the fastest ticket to getting Andreas Kostas to walk out of her life. And really, no matter what she told herself in the midst of fury and pain, that was not what she wanted.

"Are you going to open the door?" she prompted.

How could laughter sound both so darn appealing and diabolical at the same time?

The Brooklyn Bridge was even more impressive up close than from afar. No question, but watching Kayla fall in love with another piece of history was even more satisfying than seeing it for himself.

Andreas marveled that it had taken him so long to come up with his current solution to both their issues. He was not usually a dense man.

His only excuse was that he got tunnel vision when he had a goal in sight. She was a friend, he'd been blind to other options, so focused on the final steps of proving to his father and the rest of the Georgas clan that Andreas could succeed without them. He'd not realized how well that goal fit with the only other long-term one that mattered. That of keeping Kayla Jones in his life.

She pulled her phone out and smiled, typing something with her fingers, taking a picture of the bridge, typing something else and then sliding it back into her pocket.

"This is just so amazing. The ingenuity of design, the aesthetics." Her deeply appreciative sigh warmed him, though he was still irritated she was texting someone else on *their* date.

"Do you want me to get a picture of you here?" he asked, his tone even.

See him not even mention the texting.

She looked around, biting her lip, clearly torn. "It's so busy."

"We'll wait as long as it takes to get a good shot."

Her smile was worth his promise and the patience he'd promised.

"I want another one in the middle of the bridge, okay?" she asked when they were done.

"Sure."

Her phone buzzed as he handed it over. She looked down, a small tilt of her lips saying she liked whatever she saw on the screen. She typed something again.

Andreas felt a frown forming. Whom was she talking to? He didn't ask, striving manfully to respect boundaries.

She should appreciate his restraint.

They started their walk across the bridge, needing to stop every few feet for another perfect picture of the view, or the structure, and more than once she wanted him to allow her to take his photo too. She also continued texting with someone.

They reached midway and she wanted another photo, this time *with* him. "You take it. You have longer reach, you'll get more of the bridge in."

He grabbed her phone, sliding his finger over the pattern that would unlock it. It was still open to the text app from her last message.

She was chatting with that damn actor. Who else would have the screen name OnBroadway?

Another man might have clicked out of the app. But Andreas's respect for boundaries only went so far. It was not as if she had never read his texts before and vice versa. If she didn't want him reading her messages, she should have shut the app before handing him her phone.

Andreas scrolled up to scan the discussion.

OnBroadway: My sister showed me a steamy pic.

Codergirl: Your sis needs to mind her own biz.

OnBroadway: Looks like you and the boss man are friends again.

Andreas smiled to himself. And then some. The ride in the back of the private cab had gone even better than he had anticipated when he'd closed the privacy screen. But then the passion between them had always been incendiary. It had taken every ounce of Andreas's self-control not to demand the driver take them to the hotel, instead of getting out at the bridge.

Codergirl: I guess we never stopped.

Well, at least she admitted their relationship wasn't something that could simply stop at the click of her fingers.

OnBroadway: That's so sweet.

Andreas grunted.

Codergirl: Don't mock.

OnBroadway: My sister's mad at you.

Codergirl: Andreas isn't happy with you either.

OnBroadway: Maybe we should all get together for a meal while you're in town.

"No way in hell!"

Andreas would share a table with the man who had designs on Kayla the day he changed his name back to Georgas and gave his wealth away to his cousins.

Kayla grabbed his wrist of the hand with her phone in it. "What are you doing? Are you reading my texts?"

"We are not going on a double date with Jacob and his sister." He gave Kayla a look to let her know he was serious about this. "I have no interest in the woman and you have none in the brother."

"Are you sure, Andreas? I'm pretty certain she would tick all of Genevieve's boxes for you."

"I told you, Genevieve and her boxes are no longer an issue for me."

"I see."

"And you aren't interested in that Broadway actor." He needed to hear her confirm that. It shouldn't be too hard for her to do, not after what they'd done in the car.

"I'm not, am I?" she asked, her tone teasing, her expression assessing.

"You are not." He was nothing but serious.

The little tease laughed.

He felt his temper rise and opened his mouth to remind her just who she had been showing interest in, in the not-so-distant past, but her expression shifted, went thoughtful and soft.

She placed her fingertip on his lips. "No, Andreas, I'm not interested in Jacob."

"I knew you were not." That was not relief he felt, more likely heartburn from something they'd eaten at lunch.

They wouldn't be eating at that restaurant again, no matter how beautiful the view.

"Are you going to take our selfie now?"

He put his arm around her shoulder, pulling her body tight into his and did just that. He kept his arm around her after.

Kayla followed Andreas down the steps off the bridge, still reeling from what had happened earlier. His touchy-feely, all-possessive boyfriend-like behavior as they walked across the Manhattan-to-Brooklyn landmark hadn't helped her sense of unreality either.

The texts from a near stranger, who felt like a new friend, seemed like her only link to planet Earth.

"Where to now?"

"You assume I have a plan?"

"You always have a plan."

"We're going to DUMBO."

"Like the elephant?" Andreas was not a cartoon-movie guy.

He made a scoffing sound. "Like Down Under Manhattan Bridge Overpass. There's shopping." He said it like he knew that would be a selling point with her.

Of course, he was right. Even when she didn't buy anything, she loved to window-shop. "But it's the Brooklyn Bridge."

"I did not name the neighborhood."

She laughed, delighted by the tinge of annoyance in his voice, even as his hand held tightly to her own.

DUMBO turned out to be an amazing district with old converted brick warehouses now filled with living space, shops and restaurants. Some of the streets were cobbled, old freight-train tracks interspersed amid the stones.

They were browsing in a bookshop, Andreas lost in the DIY section, his guilty pleasure. He read them like Kayla read romance novels, with intense fascination and no hope of experiencing the culmination of what was between the pages.

Andreas Kostas was too busy conquering the world to build his own coffee table out of pallets, much less enjoy having such a thing in his living room. Kayla didn't foresee herself ever getting her happily-ever-after with the man of her dreams either.

Her phone buzzed with another text.

OnBroadway: You never answered my last text.

Codergirl: Andreas wasn't keen.

More like no way, no how, but she figured Jacob would get the subtext. He'd met Andreas, after all.

OnBroadway: He wouldn't be.

Codergirl: He wants to work on our friendship.

OnBroadway: Looks like he's working on more than friendship.

"4 for 4" MINI-SURVEY

We are prepared to **REWARD** you with 2 FREE books and 2 FREE gifts for completing our MINI SURVEY!

You'll get...

TWO FREE BOOKS &
TWO FREE GIFTS

...ust for participating in our Mini Survey!

Dear Reader,

IT'S A FACT: if you answer 4 quick questions, we'll send you **4 FREE REWARDS!**

I'm not kidding you. As a leading publisher of women's fiction, we value your opinions… and your time. That's why we are prepared to **reward** you handsomely for completing our mini-survey. In fact, we have 4 Free Rewards for you, including 2 free books and 2 free gifts.

As you may have guessed, that's why our mini-survey is called **"4 for 4".** Answer 4 questions and get 4 Free Rewards. It's that simple!

Thank you for participating in our survey,

Pam Powers

To get your 4 FREE REWARDS:
Complete the survey below and return the insert today to receive 2 FREE BOOKS and 2 FREE GIFTS guaranteed!

"4 for 4" MINI-SURVEY

1   **Is reading one of your favorite hobbies?**
☐ YES   ☐ NO

2   **Do you prefer to read instead of watch TV?**
☐ YES   ☐ NO

3   **Do you read newspapers and magazines?**
☐ YES   ☐ NO

4   **Do you enjoy trying new book series with FREE BOOKS?**
☐ YES   ☐ NO

YES! I have completed the above Mini-Survey. Please send me my 4 FREE REWARDS (worth over $20 retail). I understand that I am under no obligation to buy anything, as explained on the back of this card.

☐ I prefer the regular-print edition
106/306 HDL GMYF

☐ I prefer the larger-print edition
176/376 HDL GMYF

FIRST NAME   LAST NAME

ADDRESS

APT.#   CITY

STATE/PROV.   ZIP/POSTAL CODE

HP-218-MS17

Kayla sighed and sat down in one of the chairs provided for book browsers before replying.

Codergirl: He doesn't know what he wants.

Except she was pretty sure Andreas wanted sex. Hot, extremely satisfying sex.

It took a few seconds longer than she expected for the next reply.

OnBroadway: I think he does. Do you?

Now it was Kayla's turn to stop and think. Did she know what she wanted? In broad strokes, sure. She wanted security for her place at KJ Software; she wanted Andreas in her life. She could admit that.

But could she afford to want him? Specifically, *sex with him*.

Her phone buzzed. Another text.

OnBroadway: That silence? Maybe that's your answer.

Codergirl: ?

OnBroadway: Those words you can't make yourself say.

Codergirl: You're kind of smart.

OnBroadway: Just kind of?

Codergirl: Egotistical.

OnBroadway: Hey, my ego's taken a big enough hit because of a certain beautiful geek.

Codergirl: I'm sorry.

OnBroadway: Don't be. We're going to be good friends.

She smiled. She kind of thought they were already on their way there.

Codergirl: Andreas won't like that.

OnBroadway: Even better.

Codergirl: You're a troublemaker.

OnBroadway: I can be.

She let out a small laugh, only a little embarrassed when she realized someone might have heard. She looked around and realized Andreas was watching her, his expression brooding.

Her phone buzzed with another text and she looked at it.

OnBroadway: Just don't make the same mistake I did.

Codergirl: What's that?

OnBroadway: Being afraid to take a chance on a friend.

People said that emails and texts didn't convey emotions, but there was a wealth of feeling behind Jacob's last string of words.

Codergirl: What happened?

OnBroadway: I lost my friend and the chance at more.

"More texts from Jacob?" Andreas asked, his voice surprisingly mild, considering the tightness around his eyes and the tension filling his posture as he stood towering over her chair.

"Yes, give me a second." She wasn't leaving her new friend hanging after that kind of admission.

Codergirl: I'm sorry. You're a good guy.

OnBroadway: I have my career.

It wasn't enough, though, or Jacob wouldn't have advised her to go for Andreas. Kayla understood loneliness.

"Tell Jacob hello, but it's not safe to text and walk."

Meaning they were going to be walking again very soon.

She looked up at Andreas. "Are you bored, boss?"

His jaw went rigid. "Not your boss. We have more sightseeing to do."

"You are being rude."

"In what way?" He leaned against the wall by her chair, and he might have looked relaxed but for the jaw hewn from granite, crossed arms and muscles bunched with tension.

She waved her phone at him. "I am in the middle of a conversation."

"During our date," Andreas bit out.

What? They were on a date? How had she not realized that?

He was talking again before she could get her whirling mind to formulate an answer. "Do you see me talking on my cell? Have I sent a single text?"

"No."

"Because my attention is entirely on you."

Wow. Okay. This day was so not what she thought it had been. Nothing had been unexpected. He'd planned it as a date and all the sensuality had been part of it.

"I thought you were busy looking at DIY."

He shrugged. "I get that. I also get that you are not the one invested in repairing ties that you frayed."

But Andreas *was*. He might not love her, but Andreas cared more about their relationship than any other one in his life.

That mattered to Kayla. A lot.

"We were having kind of an intense conversation. Let me just tell Jacob goodbye."

Andreas nodded, his expression closed. He stepped away to give her privacy.

Codergirl: Off to see more sights. TTYL.

She felt a strange relief and a thrill of happiness when Andreas took her hand as they left the bookstore. He seemed to have a destination in mind, using his hold on her hand to guide her along.

For her part, she was just happy to take in all the color and texture. Tourists mixed with native New Yorkers, people moving quickly with a clear destination in mind, others stopping every couple of feet to take pictures. It was a magical mishmash of humanity.

"You are people watching again."

"I like it."

"Considering how much time you spend on computers, some might find your fascination with our species odd."

Just because she was cautious about the friends she made and the time she spent with them in no way meant people were not endlessly fascinating to her. How they interacted with each other. The way their bodies often said things differently than what they said with their mouths.

Yes, she found computers a lot easier to decode, but that didn't mean she was giving up on trying to decode her fellow human beings. "There's plenty to find odd about me, Andreas. I spent years of my childhood mute and still managed to skip grades."

He squeezed her hand, understanding wrapping around her, though no words were exchanged. Andreas was the only person she'd ever told about her past, and he'd never once made her feel like a freak because of it.

"You responded to the abandonment of your mother by shutting the world out. It was natural that refusing to speak was part of that for you. You trusted no one with your words."

He'd gotten that, when none of her social workers had. Her first foster mom had, though, and she'd been the one to draw Kayla out of her silent isolation. Only to send her back into it with the woman's death from breast cancer several years later.

"It's not the normal way to react to trauma. To just stop talking."

"You know how I feel about *normal*, Kayla."

Kayla grinned. "According to you, normal is boring."

"I refuse to allow anyone else to tell me what normal for my life is supposed to be. My father tried to tell me *normal* was a family with parents after my mother died, but what was normal about forcing me to live amid the very people who believed my mother was so beneath them, they never even spoke her name?"

"Weren't *any* of them worth getting to know?" Kayla asked.

She'd never questioned him before on his wholesale rejection of the Georgas clan, but she could not imagine it. She had no family. Not a single distant cousin to call her own. He had so many and rejected them all.

"I do not know. I refused to let anyone close enough to find out."

"And you don't regret that? Not even a little bit?"

"Why would I?" he asked with negligent arrogance.

"Andreas, don't you realize what I would give to have a single person I could call family?" She shook her head and then looked up at him. He was facing ahead, watching where they were walking. His expression hard to read in profile. "Someone I knew I could rely on to just be there?"

"You can't always rely on family. You know that."

"My mom, your mom's family...they aren't all there is. Families are there for each other. Just because we haven't lived it, doesn't mean we haven't seen it. Just look at how Bradley's family is. They are all so close. Look at Jacob's sister, she's mad at me because I ditched our date. Family."

"You think I could have had that with a Georgas cousin?" Andreas's voice was filled with mocking doubt.

But she wasn't going to back down just because he got a little snippy. "You don't know you couldn't. You don't know your dad wouldn't have given you something more than you let him."

She knew that right there might be pushing him too far, but she'd thought for a long time the biggest problem between Andreas and his father was that they were too much alike. Both as stubborn as each other. Both arrogant. Both sure they knew what was right.

And for a time in Andreas's life, Barnabas Georgas had the power to impose his will on his son. Without a true father-son relationship to temper that imposition, all it did was make Andreas despise the man more than he already did for the way Barnabas had treated Melia Kostas.

No attempts to make things better were going to work because Barnabas Kostas had irreparably damaged his bond with his son from the very beginning.

Andreas stopped in front of a glass building they'd seen from the boat on their harbor tour.

He turned to face her, no problem seeing how he was feeling now.

An expression of stunned disbelief tinged with anger covered his face. "Are you kidding me? That asshole did nothing but what he wanted and only for the benefit of his own consequence."

"He was spoiled. Used to getting his own way. I doubt he knew any other tactic but the one he took with you."

"His loss."

"One I bet he feels to this day."

"You don't really believe that."

She sighed. "I don't know, okay? But it's possible. Maybe there was more going on than you realized. He went about it all wrong, but maybe he didn't know how to deal with a son who hated his guts before they ever met."

"I had reason."

"I know you did." Barnabas Georgas had given Melia Kostas money for an abortion and to leave Greece.

She'd been ostracized by her family when she would only do one of those things, rejected by the man she'd loved, but she'd kept her son and raised him to the best of her abilities. And from all accounts, Melia had been an amazing mom.

"But circumstances change. People change. They learn to regret choices they made."

She'd often wondered if her mom had ever regretted abandoning her. She'd always assumed the answer was no. After all, in order to contact Kayla, all she'd had to do was go through social services.

"What is going on here, Kayla?" Andreas asked. "Why are you saying these things?"

"I'm talking to you like a friend."

"We've been friends for eight years. You've never said anything like this to me before."

"I've never felt like I could."

"Why now?"

"I'm not holding back anymore." Besides, if his animosity for his family was enough to drive him into hiring someone like Genevieve, then it wasn't healthy for Andreas to hold on to that grief so tight.

He might not see it that way, but Kayla wanted her friend happy, not trapped in a life where everything he did was to prove himself to a family he claimed to despise.

Andreas was silent for several seconds, but then his lips tilted up in a half smile, the expression in his gorgeous green eyes still solemn. "I like you being honest with me. It will take some getting used to, this no-holds-barred approach to you sharing your opinions with me, though."

"I've always been honest with you."

"But perhaps not so forthright."

She couldn't deny that she'd held back a lot. Her love, for one.

He turned toward the building, tugging on her hand. "Are you ready?"

"For what?" But then her eyes registered what was inside the glass enclosure.

A vintage carousel. Beautifully hand-painted horses on brass poles in all the traditional colors covered the circular platform, their livery done in jeweled tones, the artistry both garish and magnificent.

"You want to go on a merry-go-round?" she asked, disbelief washing over her even as she was wholly charmed.

He grinned. "Who doesn't want to ride a carousel?"

She looked around them, making a production of examining his back.

"What are you doing?"

"Looking for evidence of the pod-person replacement."

"I am not a killjoy."

"You are Andreas Kostas, synonymous with *driven*, *focused* and *determined*. I was positive amusement-park rides weren't even in your vocabulary."

"As you pointed out, we are on vacation."

"I am on vacation…" Her voice trailed off for a second, Kayla searching for what to say. "You are… I'm not sure what you are doing here."

"I thought I'd made myself very clear. I'm here until you come home, hence *we* are both on vacation." The impatient, never-stands-in-a-line Andreas Kostas got in line with Kayla and waited his turn to pay for their tickets.

"So, we are going to ride a carousel." Because *that* made so much sense. Oh, and by the way, they were on a date. That was apparently part of this now-joint vacation too.

Was Kayla losing her mind, or had Andreas gone around the bend?

"Exactly." He sure didn't sound crazy, just very determined.

But determined to do what?

Kayla was shocked at how inexpensive the tickets were, in the city where even the McDonald's coffee cost more than it did back home. Delighted by the gorgeous paint job on the horse Andreas helped her climb onto, she was unsurprised when he stood beside her, rather than taking his own horse. In a way, his refusal to actually *ride* the merry-go-round helped her feel less disconnected from reality.

He stood close, an arm around her, one strong hand curled over the glistening black mane of her horse. His other hand rested on her thigh. Her body's instant reaction to his nearness, to the sensation of being surrounded by him, overwhelmed her senses.

She could barely hear the music piping through the loudspeakers over the pounding of her heart in her ears. Her skin felt too tight for her body, the need she'd thought sated in the car was suddenly roaring through her again. Her olfactory glands inundated with his scent, that special spicy musk that had only ever meant one thing to her. Andreas Kostas.

"Are you enjoying yourself, Kay-love?" he asked, his thumb rubbing a light pattern against her thigh that was driving her to distraction.

"Yes."

He chuckled. "Oh, now, that sounds promising." He leaned down, nuzzling her ear. "I love the smell of your hair."

"It's the coconut oil in my smoothing product."

"It's you."

The carousel started to slow and Andreas whispered, "You were wrong about something you said earlier."

"What?"

"You said you don't have a single person you can count on, no matter what. You do, Kayla. You have had for eight years. You have me." With that soul-destroying statement, he stepped back.

CHAPTER EIGHT

THE CAROUSEL CAME to a complete stop. Somehow, Andreas made sure she came off her horse on the side he stood on and her body pressed against his. "My mother loved the carousel in Portland. She took me often as a child."

Kayla found herself mesmerized by the look on Andreas's face as well as the glimpse into his childhood before the Georgas debacle that seemed to define so much of his adult endeavors.

"Are you sure it was your mom who liked the carousel?" she forced words past a suddenly dry throat to tease. "And not a small boy named Andreas who liked riding the horses?"

Andreas's smile was something so special, Kayla could barely breathe. "It may have been. And now you have another secret of mine to keep."

She met his gaze, imbuing her own with as much sincerity as she could. "Your secrets are safe with me."

"Even my intransigence with my family?"

"Even that."

"Do you want to try to find your family?" he asked.

It wasn't a new question, not that he'd ever asked it, but she had asked herself that very thing many times. And she still didn't have an answer, so she remained silent as they left the carousel and started walking again.

"I don't know. She abandoned me at a truck stop, you know?" Kayla finally broke the silence between them. "Why would a mom do that? I wasn't a baby. I was three years old. I was never adopted, Andreas."

"I know that."

But did he understand what it meant? Not only had Kayla not been a child worthy of a family taking on permanently, but her long-term residency in foster care meant her own mother had never come back for her. "She could have found me, through social services, until I was eighteen. If she'd wanted to."

"No doubt the woman who gave you birth is a lost cause." Andreas's face reflected a ruthlessness few saw, but which she knew didn't bode well for whoever was on the receiving end of that look. "You might have more family besides her, though."

"If I had grandparents, aunts or uncles, wouldn't she have left me with them?"

"I do not think you can make assumptions about that, Kay-love. I have many Kostases and Georgases in Greece and while not one of them lifted a hand to claim me, to help my mother in all the years she worked so hard on her own, you cannot be certain your own mother even told her own relatives about you. They could be decent people."

Or they could be just like the woman who'd abandoned her. That was what had prevented her from hiring a private detective to find what family Kayla might have, the fear of more rejection. "So could yours."

"For me, it does not matter," Andreas dismissed. "I do not want family that rejected the woman who gave everything for me."

"Do you think they ever regretted it? Your mother's parents, I mean. They must have, after she died."

Andreas shook his head, his expression tolerant. "Your heart is so tender for a computer geek."

"Whatever." She wasn't a pushover, but Kayla wasn't the cynic Andreas was either.

"My mother invited her parents to come to America to meet me, more than once, and they refused. They maintained contact via letters only. However, they wanted to see me after Georgas acknowledged me."

"You refused them." Kayla had no doubts on that.

"Naturally."

"Your father allowed it." That surprised her.

"He never acknowledged my mother, so why would he want to recognize her family as part of my life?" Andreas asked, giving voice to Kayla's curiosity.

"But he *was* open to doing so?" she confirmed.

"He was seeking some way to cross the divide between us."

And, man, Barnabas had picked the worst possible way to do *that* particular thing. "Let me guess, it never occurred to him to simply ask you what you wanted."

"I wanted to return to America and change my name back to Kostas."

"Neither of which fit his plans to make you his heir." Barnabas Georgas had never stood a chance, for all his money and power, not when it came to his only child.

"No."

"What is he doing for an heir now?"

"I have no idea, but there are several first cousins. He's spoiled for choice, if he weren't so spoiled to having things his own way."

She almost said *Pot, meet kettle*, but knew that would hurt Andreas and that was not her intention. "Are you so sure he only came after you because he wanted an heir? It sounds like the family had that role covered."

"Not from his loins, and to a man like the Greek business shark Barnabas Georgas, that's what matters." The disgust in Andreas's voice was absolute.

But then his father had wanted Andreas aborted, so for the man to come around later looking for an heir had to have really hit Andreas on the raw.

"I get that you're convinced, and no way am I going to say your sperm donor sounds like a nice guy."

"But?" Andreas asked, his mouth a flat line, his tone mocking.

"*But* you were grieving the loss of the one person you loved in the world when Barnabas Georgas showed up in your life and came stomping in with his ugly, heavy hobnailed boots, prepared to get what he wanted by hook or by crook. He was an arrogant monster, no denial, but I'm not convinced he wasn't also a man desperate to reconnect to the son he thought lost to him forever."

"By his own choice."

"Yes, a choice he probably regretted deeply and not only because he and his wife had never been able to have children together."

"Why would you believe this?"

"Because in the beginning, he could have squashed you like a bug. He didn't do that." And she wasn't just talking about when Andreas went to Greece, but if Barnabas Georgas had wanted to crush KJ Software before they made a name for themselves, he could have done it.

He'd never even tried. He'd never tried to block Andreas getting into the university he'd wanted to. He'd done nothing to prevent his son's successes.

Maybe he was playing a long game, hoping Andreas would one day come back and play the Georgas heir, but maybe he just wanted his son to be happy and successful.

Andreas opened his mouth and then shut it again.

"How did his wife treat you?"

"She was surprisingly kind." Andreas shrugged. "I thought she would hate me, but she didn't. She didn't hate my father either."

"You thought she should."

"He cheated on her." Andreas looked baffled. "She treated him with what looked like genuine affection and he was very respectful and warm toward her."

"Do you think his relationship with your mother was an aberration?"

"It may have been. There was no evidence of other mistresses in the wings, but then he'd done a decent job of keeping my mother a secret, as well."

They'd reached the area under the bridge again by this point and for the first time in hours, Andreas pulled his phone out. He sent a text.

She gave him a questioning look.

"Calling for our car."

"The same driver?" she asked, immediate embarrassment at the idea she had to face someone who knew what she'd been doing with him in the car earlier suffusing her with heat.

"I don't know. It's a service."

"Oh."

"You blush kind of spectacularly."

Yeah, despite her dusky skin tone, she still managed to show the world when she was embarrassed. "You're not supposed to notice."

"I was unaware of that rule."

She just shook her head. "How is it that people think I'm the one who is socially awkward?"

"Because you do not recognize certain social cues. I ignore them."

"And that makes it okay?" she demanded. "It's fine for you, but not for me?"

"No double standard exists between us because I have never considered your quirks as less than and you have always tolerated my impatience with the social niceties."

"The rest of the world says you are normal, while I am not."

"The rest of the world does not matter."

A sleek black sedan pulled up, forestalling any further discussion on the matter. Kayla wasn't sure she had any more to add anyway. Andreas didn't care what others thought and she had learned long ago she couldn't let them matter too much either.

Nevertheless, she was glad to see the driver was unfamiliar.

Andreas closed the privacy screen between the back and the driver as soon as they were settled in their seats. Kayla's heart sped up, her breath catching as a curl of undeniable anticipation warred with her common sense.

She jerked her head side to side several times. "No, no, no, Andreas. We are not doing that again."

"Doing what?" he asked, devilish amusement sparkling in his green gaze.

Her fingers scrabbled for her headphones that were not there, nothing to cut out the rest of the world. Nothing to help her ignore Andreas and the maelstrom of emotions he evoked inside her. "You do not pull off innocent. At all."

"That is because I left innocent behind a long time ago."

She would have answered, in wholehearted agreement, but masculine lips pressed firmly against hers. The kiss didn't shock her this time. Not even a little. She knew it was coming. Had known it was coming since getting out of the car before crossing the bridge.

Even without the surprise factor, it still annihilated her senses.

Despite her verbal protests, she didn't fight the sensations roaring through her. There was simply no point. Whatever the rational part of her brain told her, she knew the truth deep in her soul. Kayla wanted this kiss. This moment. *This feeling*.

She *wanted* Andreas.

All rational argument against intimacy with him went up in the conflagration of desire a single touch of his mouth to her elicited.

She let herself experience it all, every amazing spark of sexual energy, each tiny zing of sensual delight. She had no idea how much of this physical intimacy she and Andreas would have…how much was on offer, much less how much she could ultimately allow herself.

But she was going to revel in every moment between them, because she knew the frozen chill of loneliness while standing beside him in the same room all too well. She knew what years of want, need, aching unfulfilled desire felt like.

She knew the deep, searing pain of unrequited love, of frustrated longing, of lust that went unsatiated so long, she almost forgot what true sexual contentment felt like.

Kayla knew what it was to hunger. She'd spent her lifetime wishing for things just out of reach, grieving losses she'd never had any control over.

In this moment she would embrace the *getting*, no matter how temporary.

This time, she didn't just hold on to him while they kissed, she explored the hard planes of his body, both remembering and rediscovering him in the most visceral of ways. Her hands skimmed over Andreas, mapping every bulging muscle, touching places she knew caused him extra pleasure. Triumph flared through her when his breath caught, his kiss growing more fervent, proving her touch was true, her memories still accurate, that she, Kayla Jones, was capable of turning this man—the only man who mattered to her—on.

When she curled her hand around his hard sex, his response was electric. Andreas's big body went rigid, his groan deep and loud.

He slid his lips from hers, along her jaw. "Careful, *pethi mou*. We will never make it to our next tourist attraction if you keep doing that."

"If you gave the driver any address but our hotel, Andreas Kostas—" she paused, her hand tightening on its cloth-covered prize, letting the seriousness of her words sink in "—I am going to infect every single one of your connected devices with an irreparable virus."

It wasn't an idle or paltry threat. She'd connected his smartphone to his tablet, which was now also linked to his work system as well as the system that controlled his home's heating, lights, etc., as well as his alarm systems. No one else could have done it, but Kayla could bring Andreas's life to a standstill.

His deep, sexy chuckle said despite the severity of her threat, Andreas was not worried.

Pulling back, she glared up at him. "You think I'm joking?"

"Oh, no, Kay-love. I am certain you would follow through." He trapped her hand where it was, even though her body was straining back, his gorgeous eyes glittering with green fire. "I have never enjoyed another woman's hands on me as much as yours."

"Do not try to sweet-talk me, Kostas. I'm not in the mood for your teasing."

"I see that." He thrust against her hand, the hard bulge under her hand more a temptation than he could possibly know.

"So?"

"Are you demanding we go back to the hotel and make love?" he asked, no mockery or even justifiable triumph in his tone, just a good dose of sexual heat.

She glared, her own frustration boiling near the surface, realizing he was calling the bluff of all her earlier denials, demanding she spell it out for him. "Are you saying you would rather do something else?"

"No." He was suddenly very serious. "There is nothing I want more."

"And the tourist attraction?"

"A joke."

"In poor taste." And maybe she was a teensy, tiny bit defensive.

"But I like when you get testy."

"You can be really annoying, Dre."

His grin was huge and very sexy, a testament to the fact he knew he had won. "I am very lucky you put up with me."

"You are, not that I think you really believe that."

"I do, though." He cupped her face, his thumb brushing along her cheekbone. "I know how very lucky I am to have you in my life. I always have done."

"You don't make any sense." She did not like when he talked in riddles.

"Because we do not see the world the same way."

No question. For all that they'd both suffered loss and pain, Andreas had always had more of a safety net. He just didn't realize it.

And that net allowed him to see the world differently than she did. Hence his ability to say that he saw her as necessary to his life, even as he was making plans for one in which she would by necessity play a smaller and smaller part.

She wasn't thinking about the future right now, though. Kayla was with the one man who had ever been able to give her everything she needed on an intimate level, most likely for the last time with any level of privacy. When they got back to Portland, he had venture capital worlds to conquer, a bride to find—with or without a matchmaker—and Kayla hopefully would still have KJ Software and the shelter she funded.

Not all she wanted, or even needed, but what she'd learned she could have.

Besides, she was on vacation, darn it. She was going to go home with memories. Memories that just might have to last her a lifetime.

"So, back to the hotel?" she asked.

"Yes, *pethi mou.* Back to the hotel, where I will ravish your body until you are ready to accept the only terms that make sense for our future."

If he thought great sex, even the best sex *they'd* ever had, was going to convince her to walk away from KJ Software and take the leap into venture capital investment, he was living in Dreamland.

Now that the decision to return to the hotel had been put out in the open, the fact they were going to make love was a given, there was a different quality to his kisses.

They turned languid and slow, but no less sexually devastating, no less emotionally catastrophic. His lips possessed hers, demanded she returned in kind. His tongue tasted, teased her into tasting.

And what he tasted like was *hers*, for that moment anyway.

They arrived at the hotel sooner than she expected, but not as quickly as she needed. She wanted skin-on-skin contact. She'd been without his touch for too long. She wanted to touch him without hindrance, craved his hands on her body with nothing in the way, as well.

But when they reached their suite, he did not immediately take her into his arms. Instead, he stared at her with those deep, fathomless green eyes for long seconds.

"What?" she demanded.

"I am thinking how beautiful you are."

She made an inelegant sound of disbelief. "So beautiful you did not touch me for six years."

"I explained that."

"And now suddenly, you're not worried about losing me if you take me to bed again?" What was the matter with her?

Was she trying to talk him out of it now that she'd decided she wanted the same thing he did? But he wasn't making sense. And she hated it when things didn't make sense, especially Andreas.

"Circumstances change."

Right. He was selling the company. She wasn't going to be his very minor partner any longer. Or he was hoping that by sexing her up he'd convince her to move on from KJ Software with him. Either way, the situation balanced in his business-literal brain.

She shrugged off her jacket, her breath catching at the way his eyes zeroed in on her hard peaks as they strained against her tank top. Tight and aching for another kind of stimulation, her nipples tingled under his hot gaze. She had always loved the way he looked at her in this mood, the way his gaze on her body could be almost a tactile sensation.

It wasn't enough, though. Not nearly enough. She wanted more; she wanted real touch and lots of it.

Putting her hands on the hem of her tank top, she gave him a flirtatious look, knowing just what the combination would do to *Mr. Control.* "Like what you see, Andreas?"

"You know I do." His voice came out more growl than billionaire-businessman tone.

Ooh, she liked it when that happened.

"How much?" she prodded, tugging up a little on the top, showing just a small line of skin above her waistband, teasing him…teasing herself.

Finesse and control disappearing in a husky breath, Andreas ripped his own shirt off, his slacks going next with swift, almost jerky, movements, revealing his hard sex barely contained by the black briefs he still wore. "This much."

She gasped, her reaction to his body visceral and intense. She knew he kept in shape with daily workouts and martial arts, but his broad shoulders layered with lean muscle, sculpted chest and eight-pack abs were totally droolworthy. He'd always looked more like a warrior than a corporate shark to her.

Only six years ago, his body had been that of a young man, but he'd filled out more, his body nothing less than awe inspiring now.

"I have always gotten off on the way you look at me, Kay-love." Andreas's tone was every bit as deep and smoldering as his green gaze.

"I'm sure you've had plenty of women look at you the same way."

"No." His denial was too sincere for her to disbelieve him. "No one has ever looked at me with the same intense desire, not like you. Your eyes make me burn."

"Good."

"Oh, yes, very."

She pulled her tank top a little farther up, loving the feel of his eyes on her, so intimate, so knowing, almost as good as a touch, as they followed the hem of her top. "It's the same for me."

"I know." His hands curled at his sides, like he wanted to reach out and grab her, but was stopping himself.

"Arrogant." She could barely get the single word past her suddenly tight throat.

"The truth is not arrogance."

Maybe not. She didn't have the breath or the focus to argue with him regardless.

Only one thing was on her mind right now, and it wasn't semantics. She removed her top, slowly, because she knew it would drive him crazy the longer she took.

His growl was very satisfying. "No one could appreciate your beauty as much as I do."

"Are you saying I am only sexy to you?" She paused with her hands behind her back on the clasp of her bra, again teasing him with what was to come, taunting him with her words and the prospect she might stop undressing.

"No," he said forcefully. "I am saying that chemistry plays a part here, Kayla. You understand chemical reactions."

"Yes." She unclasped her bra and knew by the flaring of his nostrils he noticed the sound, but she didn't let the lingerie fall away. "I do."

He took a step toward her, but stopped, his pupils already blown with passion, his jaw clenched. "What you might have with another man would be a reaction, what we have is a nuclear explosion."

She could not deny it. She'd always believed that was because she loved him. He thought it was because they had some kind of extra chemical attraction. She almost shook her head at him, but right now she really didn't care why they were so explosive together. All that really mattered was that they were.

"Oh, yes," she said as she let her bra fall away from her generous curves.

Andreas swore in Greek before reaching out to cup her breasts, his fingers brushing over her nipples with unerring accuracy, making her gasp and shudder. "Your body was made for mine."

She had no answer for a claim that he had made before and to her had always sounded more permanent than she knew he meant it to. Back then she'd been naive and believed the implications, now she had the benefit of a learned past to teach her his words were nothing but impassioned sex talk.

He leaned down and nibbled along her ear, making Kayla shiver with desire. "My sweet, *pethi mou*, what do I have to do to get you take off those too-damn-sexy slacks that cling to your butt like a second skin?"

"You want me to take these off?" she forced herself to tease in a voice made breathy with desire. Despite wanting to make love with Andreas more than she wanted to keep breathing in the moment, Kayla could not afford to give in too easily, on anything.

Andreas never appreciated anything he got too

easily, and she was determined he would remember this, their last time together, as something special. She would be the one who got away, the one he never forgot.

Because she was never going to forget him.

"I do." He tugged at her earlobe with his teeth, sending all sorts of sexy messages along her nerve endings.

"You've already taken off your slacks…" She paused to take a much-needed breath. "I suppose…" She tried again, "I suppose it's only fair."

"You are a fair person," he praised as he pinched her nipples just enough to bring pleasure, rolling them between thumbs and forefingers.

"I try to be."

He kissed along her neck. "You have always helped me with my lack in that area."

She nodded. Andreas had once told her that he considered Kayla his backup conscience. Maybe she should have taken heed he considered he needed one. She might not have been so blindsided by the events of the past two days.

She unbuttoned and unzipped, but didn't take it any further, too enamored by the sensations this buildup to pleasure was giving her. And maybe just a little too breathless. "You sure this is what you want?"

"Continue to tease me at your peril, woman." But he made no move to undress her himself, his hands fully occupied with her breasts, his body hot and hard against hers.

She undulated against him, rubbing her bare stomach against his still-covered erection. "But teasing is what you like, my darling Dre."

He groaned, one hand snaking around her to grind her into his body possessively. "Say that again."

"You like being teased. We both know it." The only thing he liked better was teasing her to the point of incoherence.

"Not *that*."

She had to stop and think, her brain not functioning on optimum at that moment. "You want me to call you 'my darling Dre' again?"

"Yes."

Oh, that was definite. She'd never used endearments with Andreas back in the day. She hadn't felt confident enough to despite his dropping things like *"pethi mou"* and "Kay-love" into conversation. She'd been afraid if she did, it would reveal the depth of her feelings.

But now, well, the words just felt flirty…right. And maybe she didn't want to keep hiding everything so perfectly. After all, hiding her every inclination before hadn't managed to save her relationship.

"My darling Dre, is this what you want?" she asked as she wiggled the teal pants down her hips, kicking her shoes off and stepping out of the fabric in the same set of movements.

She stepped back, away from his touch, straightened and cocked one hip, offering him a full-bodied view, allowing herself the same luxury. Unconcerned that she was not one of the supermodels who had graced his arm in the past six years, Kayla took in every inch of Andreas's glorious body, pushing away any nerves, no room for such between them.

The way his gaze roamed down her womanly figure, stopping at her breasts for significant time and then again at the apex of her thighs, said that he approved the view of her in only the matching peach silk panties with lace insets to the bra she'd discarded earlier.

"You still have a weakness for the store with the pink-striped bags, I see," he drawled in a low, sexy tone.

She shrugged, some devil inside her prompting her to taunt, "Maybe Jacob helped me pick them out yesterday."

CHAPTER NINE

KAYLA'S SILLY JOKE had a totally unexpected response.

The sound that came out of Andreas was wholly primal, unquestionably angry and matched with fire sparking in his green gaze. He was across the room so fast, she had no time to prepare, before he swept her up into his arms, and yet she felt not a single frisson of fear as he carried her into his bedroom.

He stood beside the giant California-king bed for several tense seconds, his jaw hewn from granite. "You did not buy the lingerie for the actor."

"Are you so sure?" She hadn't, but she could have.

She could have bought any manner of lingerie for any number of men in the past six years, and it was just registering with her how much that would have bothered Andreas. Irrational, much?

"What? Do you expect me to live celibate while you are out shopping for your perfect bride?" she demanded.

"No." He laid her on his bed, yanking the royal blue down duvet back as he did so in a truly impressive feat of coordination. He trailed his forefinger along the waistband of her panties. "So pretty. Not bought yesterday." Only there was this expression in his eyes that said just maybe he wasn't as certain as his tone implied.

"I've had this set for more than a year, Andreas.

You're the only man who's ever seen them." She grabbed his hand and laid it right over her silk-covered mound. "The only one who has ever touched them."

"Good." Possessive satisfaction flared in his green gaze, his hand pressing down and sending a thrill of desire and need through her. "I like knowing that more than I can say."

More than he *should* say, that was for sure. "You haven't been celibate for the past six years."

"Neither have you."

She didn't answer. She might as well have been.

One fingertip slipped under the leg band of her panties and brushed ever so gently over her most intimate flesh. "I've been too damned busy building our company to sleep with as many women as the tabloids claim, Kayla, you know this."

She turned away from his too intense look, dipping her head in acknowledgment. So, he hadn't slept through half the Portland population of beautiful women, but that didn't make her feel any better about the ones he *had* taken to his bed.

He pressed between her nether lips, caressing slick flesh and performing a gentle whorl on her clitoris, evoking sensations both deep and intense through the core of her. "Hey, *pethi mou*. It is you here with me now. It is me here with you. That is what matters."

She met his emerald gaze, her heart beating so fast, she could feel it in her throat, her breath coming out in short pants. "Is it?"

"It is." He kissed her, his lips molding to hers with perfect pressure, cutting off words and thoughts.

Somehow, she lost the last piece of disputed lingerie. His briefs disappeared, as well. Both at Andreas's hands because Kayla was too busy touching skin, kissing lips and trying to press her body up into his. His big, hard sex rubbed against her hip as he drew pleasure from her body in ways it hadn't experienced in six long years.

Whether it was the fact she was older and her body had changed or that she had gone all that time without knowing the fullness of these feelings, *everything* was stronger than she remembered. Everywhere his naked body touched hers sent pure jolts of electric ecstasy directly to her core. Her nipples rubbed against the hair on his chiseled chest and it made her wetter, hotter, needier than she'd ever been.

Seconds melted into minutes and Kayla ached with the need to have Andreas inside her.

"Tell me you're clean," she demanded with one of her few remaining lucid thoughts.

He shook his head, like he was trying to clear it. "What?" he demanded, his voice husky and gruff.

"You're clean. Tell me." He'd always been careful. That wouldn't have changed in six years, not with women who meant nothing to him.

He stared down at her like he was still processing her words, but then his expression cleared. "You know I take care of myself. I have the results of my last tests on my phone."

"Me too." They needed to stop. So she could see his, show him hers.

She'd never had sex without that safety check. Not even the first time with Andreas.

No amount of pleasure was worth risking her life.

Only, her body was telling her to forget it, to just keep with the pleasure. Her heart was telling her he would never, ever lie to her or put her at risk, and her brain…it wanted to get on the crazy train and just look later.

But then Andreas jumped off the bed.

She made a very embarrassing sound of need. "Where are you going?"

"To take care of you." He grabbed his phone and then shoved it at her. "Read it."

She glanced at the screen, saw the familiar logo from his doctor's office, while her heart said a very loud and resounding *I told you so* to her brain. "Okay."

"You didn't even open the lab results." He reached out and traced her jawline. "I mean it. You will take care of yourself. You will confirm this fact."

"I trust you, Andreas." And she did, about this. More than she would trust any other man.

"I am glad, but you will read the test results nevertheless. This is nonnegotiable."

No matter how much he wanted her, and the leaking tip of his fully engorged hard-on told her it was a lot, he was going to make sure she was taken care of in every way.

Like he always did.

She clicked into his app for his doctor's office and read his latest test results. All good. Just like he'd said. She pulled her own up on the same app since they had the same clinic, if not the same doctor, and showed him hers.

His smile was gorgeous and full of heat.

"I had no doubts."

"Now, can you please sex me up?" she asked maybe just a little petulantly.

"You want me inside you?"

Was he kidding? "Like yesterday!"

His laughter was rich, warm and oh, so sexy. "Yesterday, you would have thrown your phone at my head if I suggested naked games in my bed."

"Less talking, more with the touching." Okay, so he was right, but seriously? Weren't men the ones who were supposed to have one-track minds?

Finally. He came over her, his hard sex rubbing against her wet, swollen, intimate flesh, drawing a moan of pleasure from her. His skin was silky and hot against hers...his sex so hard, so good. She'd almost forgotten how good this could be. How? And how could she have settled for less?

"I don't want to use a condom," he groaned, sounding a little embarrassed, but mostly just really, really turned-on.

Her entire body suffused with desire at his lust-filled words. Kayla's computerlike brain made the mental calculations. The risk of pregnancy was as low as it could get without birth control.

Still, he needed to know. "I'm not on anything."

"It is your choice, Kay-love."

She'd never had sex without a condom. Not even back in the day with him. She'd been on the pill, but he hadn't wanted any risks.

"Yes."

"You are certain?"

"Yes."

He nodded. His expression serious, filled with primal desire.

He did not ask again, but gently pushed inside, rocking his engorged shaft into her inch by inch, joining their bodies in intimate unity and a pleasure so intense, she felt reality fall away.

It shouldn't make so much difference, the lack of that one small barrier, but it did. They'd never done this before, never been *this* intimate. She felt the connection to him go all the way through to her soul. In that moment of joining, she knew giving in to her desire had been the biggest mistake of her life because she would never get over this man.

Kayla would never be able to settle for another lover on a permanent basis. She would never love another as she loved Andreas Kostas.

He would always own her heart, as he owned her body now in a way no ever had.

And whether he realized it, or not, she owned his.

Because no way could a connection this deep go only one direction. She didn't fool herself into believing it was permanent, but it was profound. For both of them.

The sheer rigidity of his jaw, the depths of his green gaze, they said this merging of their bodies was something *more* for Andreas, as well.

They moved together, slowly at first, the pleasure so intense and different and incredibly special until suddenly she needed more and so did he. His thrusts were hard and fast, her body meeting his with equal fervor and passionate need. They rutted together in animalistic need, while their souls intertwined around them in a spiritual ecstasy Kayla knew she would never experience with another.

Ecstasy spiraled inside, tighter and tighter, her limbs felt tight and loose at the same time, electric sparks buzzing under her skin.

He praised her in a mixture of English and Greek, telling her she was the sexiest woman he'd ever had, the best lover, tightest, best connection, that she felt better than anything he'd ever known. He demanded her pleasure and she gave it to him.

Every bit of pleasure and joy she was capable of.

"You are so beautiful in your pleasure, *pethi mou*." Andreas grabbed her hips and tilted her pelvis up, then changed his angle of thrust, doing a twist with his hips when his pelvis met hers.

"I love…what you are doing to me!" she cried, holding back the word she wanted to say, knowing the admission would be unwelcome.

The new sensations sent her into final sexual overload, her body convulsing with a climax of cataclysmic proportions she could no more hold back than stop loving Andreas.

She arched up toward him, her muscles locked in a rictus of delight, her scream loud and long, his name coming out on a wail. "Andreas!"

"That is right, Kay-love. Mine. You are mine."

His possessive words washed over her, increasing her pleasure, his knowing touch on her body prolonging her climax even as she felt him join her in orgasm. And as she felt the heat of his come inside her for the first time, she had a second climax, her womb contracting, her body's response to that perfect sensation.

As Kayla came apart for a second time below him, Andreas shook from the aftershocks of his own mind-blowing climax. He hadn't just come, he'd had a near out-of-body experience. Nothing like sex was supposed to be. Easy. Stress reducing, but nothing special.

It had never been that simple with Kayla. He'd had other lovers, but not one of them had come close to turning him inside out like she did.

Ecstasy still coursed through him, locking his muscles, making his heart pound, his blood hot in his veins, a one-word refrain repeating over and over again in his brain. *Mine.*

She was his. She had to see that now. See how this, them together in the same bed, was inevitable.

He finally saw it. It had taken him six years, but Andreas finally got it.

Kayla was meant to be his. Not just his business partner. Not just his family by default because she was his best friend, but the woman who would make his plan to prove his value, his plans for the future, happen.

She made that small postcoital whimpering sound that had always driven him wild. "Andreas."

Nothing more, just his name, but in that breathy tone? With that sated expression on her beautiful café au lait face? It was all he needed. He would convince her that their futures were entwined.

There was no other choice.

He'd made her see six years ago that they needed to go into business together. Now he would convince her that marriage was the next logical step for them. Because not being in each other's lives, that was not an option.

Twisting his hips and pressing down, he drew out the dregs of their pleasure, pulling a moan from her, his own sexual satisfaction so deep he had to bite back a growl. "This is right, Kay-love. Admit it."

She gasped, looking at him with liquid gray eyes.

He kissed her, demanding her body's agreement with his lips. Her hips cradled him so perfectly, her mouth so soft against his own, the kiss surprisingly passionate considering what they had just done and how they had both come so spectacularly.

But his body was not done, his hard-on never growing soft despite his climax, and within moments of the beginning of their passionate kiss, he was moving his hips again. Taking his time on this round, he drew out their pleasure, rubbing their bodies together even as he pressed in and drew out of her velvet heat in a rhythm as old as time, but that felt like something altogether new, just between them.

Kayla moved against him, her hands on his body, touching him with instinctual knowledge of what would enhance his pleasure. She tugged him closer to her, like she wanted to meld their skin together, amping up his arousal.

Her desire for him was an aphrodisiac all on its own.

This time when she climaxed, her cry was soft and raw, her hands clutching his back, her nails digging into his skin. He reveled in the small pain as he came inside her, knowing that though chance was small, there *was* a chance they had a made a child together. That knowledge increased his own bliss tenfold, forcing a primal shout of victory from him.

She was his.

He smiled as her eyelids drooped, content to watch her fall asleep. She'd often done this before, napping for a few minutes to an hour after sex. And he spent the time watching her sleep. There was something intimate about this ritual, and personal, something only theirs.

He had not realized how much he had missed watching her in slumber, but something settled inside him as she showed him the ultimate trust as her entire body relaxed into unconsciousness.

He withdrew from her and rolled to the side, laying an unashamedly possessive hand over her stomach. The thought of her carrying his child was incredibly appealing. Visions of a little girl with curly black hair and gray eyes like her mama flashed in his mind's eye.

Kayla only slept about ten minutes, coming awake with a kittenish scrunching of her nose. Her gray gaze caught his in solemnity. "You're still here."

"It *is* my bed." He had brought her to his room on

purpose. He'd been making a statement, but he wasn't sure she got it.

"You stayed in it. You don't always. I'm surprised you're not in the shower already."

"Much more enjoyable to share the shower." He winked.

She didn't smile. Didn't reply, but simply stared at him with fathomless eyes. He couldn't tell what she was thinking and he didn't like it.

Without more discussion, he got up and lifted her out of the bed.

She yelped. "Andreas, what do you think you are doing?"

"Carrying you to the shower."

"I can walk!"

"I never doubted it." He nudged the large en suite bathroom's door open with his shoulder.

The oversize glass-encased shower was nearly as big as the one in his condominium back in Portland, sufficient space enough for two, especially if they didn't mind getting close. And as far as he was concerned, that was the whole idea. He had always enjoyed washing her body, the intimacy of it something that touched him on a level he would never speak about, but it was especially good after they made love.

He felt like he was taking care of her.

She was so independent, there were few instances she allowed him to do so.

But in the shower, with several showerheads sending heated water cascading over both of them, Kayla allowed him to minister to her body, going soft in a way she so rarely did outside the bedroom.

This time, she stood stiffly at first and he was worried something had changed too much in their dynamic in the intervening six years between being lovers, not lovers and lovers again. She grabbed the luxurious natural loofah that came packaged new in both their bathrooms and put a spicy scented shower gel on it.

But when she went to wash herself, Andreas tugged the loofa from her hand. "Let me."

She stubbornly clung to it, staring up at him, her gray gaze unreadable.

"We will both enjoy our shower more if you allow me to wash you."

Her luscious lips twisted in an unhappy moue. "That's what I'm afraid of."

"Why be afraid?"

"You would not understand."

It was she who did not understand. "There is nothing to fear here, Kayla. Trust me."

Their gazes locked, hers weighing his, and he felt his very soul was being weighed in the balance. Finally, she released the loofa, but the wary expression on her beautiful face bothered him more than he wanted to admit.

Kayla had always trusted him. Why suddenly was she doubting his intentions?

He washed her body with infinite care, not being overtly sexual, but incapable of being purely platonic either. He stopped using the loofa and soaped his own hands to wash/caress every inch of her. No question. Her body was everything tempting to him.

It always had been, but now that he'd tasted her skin again, had lain between her legs and known the ultimate pleasure, there was no way he would ever look at her again without feeling at least a tinge of desire. He didn't know how he'd managed the platonic relationship for six years, looking back on it.

When she gave a breathy little gasp and sagged

against his body, he didn't even try not to touch her intimately. She wanted more pleasure, it was in the very air around them. He could do nothing but give it to her.

He pulled her against him, nestling her bottom against his renewed erection, and cupped her generous curves. "You are so perfect here. I love your breasts, *pethi mou*."

He tweaked her nipples and she cried out. The sounds of her pleasure went through him, setting off a chain reaction in his libido, telling his body to ready for claiming her body yet again. He had not been a teenager in years, but damn, he was hornier than a mindless adolescent getting his first taste of sex. He craved her like a drug.

"Again?" she asked breathlessly.

He let one hand slide down, his middle finger dipping between her legs, pressing against her clitoris, rubbing against the slick folds. "Yes, again. Say you want it."

"I want it." No hesitation. She didn't demur or tease.

And he was damn grateful.

He spun her around and lifted her, pressing up into the warm, tight wetness of her body with as much eagerness as if they had not just made love twice already in his bed. Her arms and legs latched around him, the hot water cascading around them as once again their bodies joined in that ancient rhythm that brought forth primitive pleasure nothing else could duplicate.

Afterward, he carefully washed away the evidence of their lovemaking, cleaning both their bodies while she acquiesced with a sweetness born of sexual lethargy.

He nuzzled her neck as he reached around her to turn off the water. "We are perfection together."

"Yes." She didn't sound particularly happy about that truth.

He did not understand why, but then he'd understood very little of her actions since she walked out of the meeting with him and Genevieve.

He tugged her from the glassed enclosure. "Come, let me dry you."

"I can dry myself." But she made no move to grab a towel.

He smiled, inviting her to join in the pleasant afterglow, rather than wherever her thoughts had taken her. "I know, but *you* know how much I enjoy this."

"You don't seem like the kind of guy who would enjoy pampering his lovers."

"You are the only one." He had never showered with another sex partner, much less dried her off afterward in an effort to care for her needs.

Kayla went still. "I am?"

"Yes." He began drying her delectable body. "So beautiful."

"So you keep saying."

"Then I guess you should believe me."

"We both know I'm not one of those supermodels you date."

"You are you, which is far better."

"If you say so."

"I do."

She shook her head.

Once he'd wrapped her in the large bath sheet, he made quick work of drying his own body. "I have a proposition for you."

All the relaxed lethargy drained from Kayla's countenance and body, her mouth setting in a firm line, her body going taut. "I don't want to talk about business. I'm still on vacation."

"It has almost nothing to do with the company." He couldn't say *nothing* because if she had fallen in with his plans to move on to his next venture with him, Andreas was not sure his eyes would have been opened to how their future was supposed to go.

"*Almost* nothing?" she asked with clear distrust. She shook her head again. "No. I told you, you wouldn't sex me into your way of thinking."

"Since when have I earned your suspicion like this?" he demanded, an unfamiliar feeling gripping at his impenetrable heart.

It might have been hurt.

"Don't be disingenuous, Andreas."

"I am not. We have always been able to trust each other, Kayla. That has not changed."

Clear pain twisted her features. "Hasn't it?"

"No." Could she doubt it?

"We just made love." She said it like an accusation. "Three times."

"It was fantastic."

She rolled her eyes. "Yes."

"Do not roll your eyes at me. How many people in the world do you think have sex as good as what happens when our bodies are joined?"

"You think what we have is so special?" she asked with patent disbelief.

"You don't?" he demanded.

"Then how could you just turn it off six years ago?"

"I explained that."

"Yes."

"I made a mistake." He'd been looking for the wrong kind of permanence with her, but then he hadn't been ready for this step in his life then. Taking a wife wasn't on his agenda six years ago, taking a business partner had been.

"What? What are you saying? *You* made a mistake?" She sounded and looked shocked.

"Come. We'll have this discussion in the comfort of the bedroom." He didn't wait for her agreement, but led her to one of the armchairs by the window.

Once she sat, he knelt on the pristine white carpet beside her, unbothered by his own nakedness, but absurdly grateful her delectable body was covered by the bath sheet. They would never get this discussion off the ground if his libido didn't take a break, and an entirely naked Kayla would be too much of a temptation to deal with.

"I'm not discussing business. I mean it, Andreas." Oh, she sounded cranky.

He almost smiled. "I believe you. Now, will you believe me that what I wish to talk about is more personal than business?"

"Personal?" Her voice came out in a funny little very un-Kayla-like squeak.

"Yes, personal."

Kayla pulled her legs up so her arms could wrap around her knees in the large armchair, a very self-protective pose, if she knew it. "Okay, I'll listen."

"That is all I can ask."

She gave a bark of laughter. "Don't kid yourself, Andreas. We both know whatever it is, you're going to expect my cooperation. I'm just warning you, I'm done being a pushover where you are concerned."

"I have never considered you all that malleable." If anything, she was the one person who could check him, whom he would listen to criticism from.

She didn't answer, just made a *proceed* motion with her hand, before clasping it with the other tightly around her curled legs once again. Oh, she might listen, but this wary Kayla was certainly in a different place than the friend he was used to.

"One of the reasons you were so upset about my hiring Genevieve was because you believed you would of necessity be pushed from my life. Is that correct?" Despite her actions of running off to New York to make some kind of subdeal with Sebastian Hawk, Andreas and Kayla's friendship was important to her too.

Realization of that fact was very comforting to him.

Kayla's lovely full lips twisted. "Yes."

"You believe I should spend my off-hours with my wife." If that wife was not his best friend, he still wasn't sure he bought the premise, but it was clear Kayla did.

"Yes." Definitely cranky again.

And why that should spark a renewal of his libido, he had no idea, but then Kayla had always affected him differently than other women. What he would normally have no patience for he found absolutely essential in her.

Kayla noticed, her eyes widening and then narrowing with a frown. "If we're going to have this discussion of yours, could you put something on, please?"

"Of course." He went to get one of the hotel's lavish terry robes.

It did not bother him a bit that his nakedness was as distracting for her as hers would have been for him. It gave him hope.

Belting the robe, he said, "Even now you do not trust me not to allow you to be pushed aside."

"You've got your plans." Shrugging, Kayla looked away. "You're on a schedule."

"Plans that include marriage and a family." Was she still not getting it?

"Yes." This time the word sounded torn from her, not annoyed, but pained.

Again. Still. It did not matter which.

He wanted that pain gone. Now. "There is a simple solution to both our dilemmas."

"You think so?" She was looking at him again, her eyes molten silver and blazing with anger.

Anger he did not understand, but was just as determined to extinguish as the pain. "I know it."

"What is this *simple solution*?" Her concrete disbelief in him having *any* solution that would appease her was written into every lovely aspect of her face.

He would prove his problem-solving skills were up to the task. "Marry me."

CHAPTER TEN

KAYLA'S LIMBS WENT *KERSPLUNG*, her arms flailing of their own accord, her legs shooting off the chair, nearly taking the rest of her body with them. Shock deprived her lungs of oxygen as the towel she was covered with fell away at her body's jerky movements.

"What?" she demanded, absolutely sure she was hearing things.

Deep emerald eyes widened at her reaction, Andreas dropping to his knees beside her chair again. "It is the only thing that makes any sense."

Even fully covered by the luxurious robe, he was still a risk to her equilibrium. If the topic of their conversation hadn't been so shocking, she would have lost her train of thought with his nearness. Andreas Kostas as a friend was dangerous to her heart and sanity, but this close? This intimate? He was pure kryptonite.

"No… You don't know what you're saying." She grabbed at the bath sheet, pulling it back around her, pulling her knees back up, curling into herself and staring at him with near hatred for making her hope when she knew he didn't mean it. "You're not being serious."

"Believe me." Warm, masculine hands covered her now-cold fingers and squeezed. "I have never been more so."

"But, Andreas, Genevieve would never approve of me for you."

"I fired Genevieve."

"That's not the point."

"What *is* the point?" His thumbs caressed her chilled hands, seducing her with warmth.

"You don't want to marry me." If he had, he would have done so six years ago. Right?

She'd finally come to terms with the truth of their relationship. He couldn't turn everything on its head. Not now.

"But I do." His smile was as close to self-deprecating as she'd ever seen on this arrogant Greek-American's features. "I think you'll realize if you consider it that you will find marriage to me a good thing."

Was he kidding? He was the one person she'd always wanted to call family, but this made no sense. And she said so. Again.

"On the contrary, it makes all kinds of sense."

"Oh, really?" she managed to snark past her very slowly dissipating shock. "How is that?"

His smile was devastating. "We are already family. This would simply make it official."

Did he really believe that? The expression of sincerity in his emerald gaze said he did.

She shook her head. "But you wanted a bride pimp. For the *perfect wife*."

"You fulfill every one of my requirements."

"Requirements?" He had requirements? Wasn't that kind of clinical? Did he think marriage was a business contract?

Clearly, the answer was *yes*.

"Preferences. However you want to put it."

Yes, to Andreas, any preference he evinced, he would

consider in reality to be a requirement. Kayla almost had it in her to pity Genevieve if she'd kept the position of matchmaker for such an exacting client.

"I don't see how."

"How what?"

"Focus, Andreas," she said with some asperity. "That I could fulfill your requirements. I don't have social position or family standing."

She didn't have any family at all, except him apparently.

He jumped up and crossed the room, coming back for the second time that day brandishing his phone. "It's all right there."

She looked down at the screen. It was opened to an interview intake form for Genevieve's matchmaking service. He'd already scrolled to the question that asked Andreas to list his top-five preferences for his future partner.

He had made a neat, succinct list.

Practical, not given to emotional displays.
Must have own career.
Must have post-high-school education.
Not Greek.
Must want children.

Kayla shook her head. "Why not Greek?" was the first thing she thought to ask.

Andreas made a sound somewhere between disgust and anger, averting his gaze for a moment before meeting her eyes again, his a window into an old torment. "When I was in Greece, forced to live with my father, forced to take his name, forced to do so many things, I heard over and over again how one day I *would* marry

a good Greek girl, someone who would do the Georgas name proud."

There was so much old pain in his taut body right
now, she couldn't have stopped herself reaching out
with one hand and sliding it into the opening of his
robe to press against his heart. "Your mother was a
good Greek girl."

"I know, but even after he decided to acknowledge
me, Georgas was never going to acknowledge that, or
his part in her downfall with her family and commu-
nity."

"So, you are determined not to give in to even the
least of his demands."

"Exactly."

Lucky for Andreas he'd never fallen in love, particularly with some beautiful Greek woman. It might have
broken him. But then, maybe that was lucky for Kayla
too, she was finally beginning to realize.

"You weren't ever looking for someone with social
standing, a family that dated back generations."

"No. Those would be Georgas standards for mea-
surement of a person's worth, not mine. I am a Kostas,
my own person."

"I can be emotional," she pointed out. She wasn't
going to pretend to be an automaton after all this time.

"You are eminently practical." Andreas sighed and
smiled. "When you aren't haring off to New York and
refusing to tell me where you are."

"I have emotions, Andreas. I am capable of love."
She knew her social awkwardness was often interpreted
as a lack in that department, or any kind of sentiment,
but the truth was nothing like that.

"Good. Then you will love our children."

She hugged her knees tighter as a thrill of hope went

through her that even six years of practice tamping it down didn't seem able to diminish. "I want to adopt out of foster care."

"I know."

She'd told him her dreams of doing so six years ago, but assumed he'd forgotten. "That's not a problem for you?" she pressed.

"No. Though I am hopeful your willingness to forego birth control today indicates an openness to trying for children with our DNA, as well. I want Melia Kostas to live on in my children."

It was such a sentimental, *emotional* thing to say, Kayla was flabbergasted. "I did the math, the chances of pregnancy during this time in my cycle were astronomically low."

"There's that practical side to your nature showing itself." His lips quirked, his green eyes filled with amusement.

"Do not laugh at me, Andreas."

"I'm not, *pethi mou*. The fact is, even a one-in-a-thousand chance remains a chance and you would not have taken it if you were unwilling to have children with me."

"I know."

"So?"

"Would you treat all our children the same?" His answer mattered, enough she would turn him down if he gave the wrong one.

Kayla had spent her entire childhood standing on the outside of the families she lived with, looking in. She would never allow that for her own children. Not if she could help it.

And she was determined to help it.

He curled both hands over hers again, scooting farther into her personal space, his body heat surrounding her. "Any child we bring into our home, any child who has reason to call me Papa, will enjoy every ounce of my protection, my support and my love. Adopted, natural or born to us within our marriage, no child of mine will ever doubt their importance to me. How can you doubt it?"

Kayla's heart just melted. Was it any wonder she'd loved this man since she knew him? Despite his corporate-shark side, he understood what really mattered.

"I guess I don't."

"Good."

She wanted to give in, but part of her still wondered how this could be real. "Why now? Why not six years ago?"

"Six years ago, I was not ready to marry."

Right. It hadn't been part of the plan right out of graduate school. "Now you are."

"It is time."

His words served as a cold reminder that Andreas was not asking her to marry him in some grand romantic gesture, but because he had a plan to prove to his overbearing father that Andreas Kostas was every bit as good, or better than he ever would have been as Andreas Georgas.

And if Kayla said no, Andreas would find a wife. One way or another.

"Come, Kay-love. Marriage between us will give you the safety and security you crave. From this point forward, no matter what business lies between us, you will know where you belong, where you have always belonged. With me." She could not doubt the sincerity of his words, but they also proved that he knew just what buttons to push to get to her.

And that helped her stay just that little bit wary. "But marriage isn't a business contract. I'm not sure you understand that."

"Is it really so different?"

"Yes." She needed him to understand that.

"If you say so, but I keep my promises. You know this. Once I sign a contract, I keep my side of the bargain, just as you will always keep yours. I do not break my word."

She knew that in business and life as she'd seen it with Andreas, he had a deep well of integrity. She could not deny his words, but still…who wanted to see their marriage likened to a business arrangement?

Andreas did, apparently. Kayla was not so enamored by the classification.

"What kind of promises are you proposing we make?" She wanted it spelled out, needed to be sure that Andreas understood the kind of commitment he would be making and what she would require him to make.

What might be just another business deal for him, though apparently with much longer duration, was her life and her chance at the family she craved.

"Fidelity, lifetime companionship, family. It will be a real marriage in every sense of the word. How could it not be?"

"I don't know. You tell me. You're the one talking about it being like a business contract."

"Because that is what I know. What I understand."

That she could believe. He'd never understood the emotional devastation he'd wreaked when he broke up with her so he could bring her on board in his fledgling company.

"What about love?" she asked.

There was that look again. Disgust warring with anger. "My mother said she loved my father. Only that love destroyed her life."

"But not all relationships blow up like theirs did," she had to point out.

"My father claimed to love his wife, but he cheated on her. I will never take a mistress, or even have a one-night stand."

"That's about integrity and commitment, not love."

"According to many they are the same thing. My father has plenty of integrity in business. It was his supposed love for my mother that gave him the freedom to cheat, to bring about her disgrace with her family."

Kayla didn't have an answer for that and she didn't need one.

Andreas was not finished. "He said he loved me, that as his son, I was precious to him, but never once did he take into account my needs, my feelings, much less a single thing I wanted. He did nothing but disrupt and destroy the life my mother worked so hard to give me. Love is an excuse people give to justify their selfishness with others, or their own bad decisions."

Her heart hurt, bleeding from the wounds his words inflicted. "I don't believe that."

"What do you know about love?"

The stark demand of the question hit her like a physical blow. Kayla nearly blurted out her six-year-old secret then, but self-preservation kept her silent. "I know that you just got through promising you would love our children, all of them."

"That is different," he dismissed with a wave of one hand. "Melia Kostas taught me how to love a child as she loved me."

And despite how his father's love had caused major havoc in Andreas's life, apparently the big bad tycoon was still unafraid to love his own children.

"But you can never love me?" She picked at the wound in her heart like a sore tooth, needing him to say the words.

"Does it matter?" he asked, sounding pained. "Doesn't what we have transcend romantic drivel?"

Transcend love? Was he serious? But she could see he was. "A man who claimed to love you might walk away from both you and his children. It happens often enough, but I will never leave you."

She took a deep breath and then spoke some of the most difficult words she'd ever said. "I'll give you my answer back in Portland."

Instead of the anger she expected, Andreas nodded. "I expected as much."

He had?

He tipped his head down and kissed her, his lips firm but gentle. "I know you, Kay-love, no matter what you may think." He tugged at the haphazard tuck at the top of the towel. "Until then, why don't we spend more time exploring the benefits of joining our lives and our bodies, hmm?"

She had no answer as her mouth was too busy kissing him back, her body too intent on getting close to his.

They made love into the evening, ordered dinner via the special room service menu only available for their floor and the one below, and then returned to Andreas's bed, insatiable lovers who had spent too long apart.

Kayla was unsurprised when Andreas insisted on accompanying her to her meeting with Sebastian Hawk. That didn't mean she had to like it.

She crossed her arms and glared up at him. "You aren't part of this deal, Andreas."

"I'm not leaving you alone to tear around New York on your own again."

"You're being ridiculously controlling."

"I am not trying to control you."

"Aren't you?"

"No."

"Then why come to the meeting?"

"Is it so hard for you to believe I want to watch out for you? You are brilliant in the lab, Kay-love, but Hawk is a shark at business."

For a man who didn't believe in love, he certainly threw the word around a lot. She couldn't decide if she liked it or it just hurt more to hear him using it, knowing there were no feelings of love behind it. "Oh, you mean like you?"

"Don't you want a shark sitting beside you?"

"Undermining my position?" She gave him a sour look. "No, thank you."

"You believe I would do this?"

"You won't?" she asked, stunned.

"You have my word."

She stared at him. Could she trust him? If she didn't, she could only give one answer to the marriage question once they got home.

Sighing, still trepidatious, but certain she had to take a leap of faith, she said, "Okay, you may come, but I mean it, Andreas. No undermining my deal with Sebastian."

Andreas didn't bother to answer, he was too busy texting Bradley to fix the reservations at the restaurant to accommodate one more person.

"Seriously? Andreas, he's probably still sleeping."

The chime of a return text said she was wrong, until she saw Andreas's wince. Yeah, the überefficient PA had not liked being woken, but she had no doubt the reservations would get updated to a table for three.

Sebastian Hawk was already at the table when Kayla and Andreas arrived at the upscale restaurant for their meeting.

He stood from the table set formally with full linens, shaking Kayla's hand first. "It's very nice to see you, Miss Jones." He turned to Andreas. "I wasn't expecting you, but I wondered at the extra place setting."

"Andreas is convinced you're going to try to eat me," Kayla said with her usual forthrightness. "And please, call me Kayla. Formality makes me nervous."

Andreas winced, but Sebastian Hawk laughed. With the warmth in his smile and gorgeous features, it was easy to see why an Arabic princess would walk away from her intended prince to marry this man.

"Then by all means, let us dispense with it. You will call me Sebastian."

"Stop flirting with her, Hawk. Your wife would not approve."

"Lina understands the difference between polite conversation and flirting, Andreas."

Andreas frowned, but took his seat after helping Kayla into her brocade dining chair. They ordered their food before Sebastian broached the subject of business. And it was then that she discovered just how dedicated Andreas was to her interests, as well as the difference between this glam restaurant and the one they'd been to for dinner.

The waitstaff here were attentive, but clearly used to

business being conducted over lunch as they handled the food service with subtle difference.

"I'm thrilled you want to stay on at KJ Software." Sebastian's handsome face creased in a genuine smile. "As far as I'm concerned, you are the reason the security software is so much above the others in the industry."

Andreas gave the other business tycoon a less-than-warm look. "She wants more than to stay on, she wants to keep her interest in the company." Andreas's tone brooked no argument.

Kayla nodded her agreement.

"Why?" Sebastian's brows drew together, his expression perplexed. "If you allowed me to buy your shares, you would be a wealthy woman. I assure you that your employment package would be commensurate with your skills and very real importance to R & D."

"It's not about the money." Kayla hadn't really considered how she was going to explain her desire to stay partial owner of KJ Software to Sebastian Hawk.

The idea of baring her soul to him did not appeal.

"It's not?" Sebastian appeared a tad disbelieving.

"Kayla has a different attachment to the company than I do," Andreas said. "Unlike me, she has no desire to start a new venture."

"You do not like change?" Sebastian was clearly still trying to understand.

"Would you sell Hawk Enterprises?" Kayla asked instead of answering.

Sebastian's expression cleared, but remained serious. "No. I would not. You're right, Kayla, sometimes it is not about the money."

"I'm glad you understand."

"I do, but I am not sure I like the idea of you retaining five-percent ownership in my subsidiary company."

"You're a possessive bastard, Hawk." Andreas didn't sound like he was insulting the other man, despite the words he used.

Sebastian shrugged. "Lina would agree with you."

"We were talking business," Kayla felt compelled to point out.

"It's a deeply pervasive personality trait." Sebastian's lips barely twisted in recognition of his admission.

Andreas leaned back in his chair, almost a relaxed pose, but his arms crossed and his features were cast in intractability. "You'll have to keep it in check in this instance. Kayla wants to keep her stake in the company and knowing that, I can't do a deal without assuring she does."

Sebastian's eyes flared with surprise, but that was nothing compared to the shock coursing through Kayla's body. She'd think Andreas was just posturing, but she knew the truth. He never said something he would not back up with action. Not in business, not in life.

It was just that she'd never considered he would lay such a condition on him selling his 95 percent. It was all she could do to hold back her gasp of disbelief.

Sebastian looked at Kayla, his dark gaze probing and speculative. "Some of my top employees in certain subsidiaries enjoy company stock as part of their bonus package. Nothing that would allow them anything like a five-percent stake in even a subsidiary, but I am not without understanding in how to best motivate performance."

"I am aware." Andreas met Sebastian's gaze squarely. "You want Kayla's brains, she keeps her stake in the company."

That was more like the argument *she* had intended to make.

"You are aware I am building up my conglomerate to have worthy companies, not simply a name to give to my children."

Sebastian gave a short nod. "You're building a damn dynasty. I am aware."

Sebastian's smile was wry. "Lina chose an American businessman over royalty. Our children will have a legacy worthy of such a mother."

Kayla shook her head. Andreas wasn't the only business tycoon with something to prove.

"So, we have a deal?" She pressed her hands tightly together under the table, still unable to believe after all her angst Andreas had come down so strongly on her side during this negotiation.

Sebastian looked at her and then back at Andreas. "I have a counteroffer."

"What is it?" Kayla asked, unwilling to allow Andreas to continue running the meeting, no matter how successful his words might have been.

"You sell half your five percent to Andreas."

"Why?" Andreas demanded.

Kayla frowned in thought. Was 2.5 percent enough to maintain her sense of security? The money would certainly come in handy for the shelter.

"You can consider it one of your first investments for your new venture capital company," Sebastian said. "So long as you own skin in the game, the new CEO will have access to your brains and industry contacts. One day, you'll be there to help mentor my children."

No matter how much Kayla might like the idea, Andreas would never go for that. It wasn't part of his grand plan and he never gave up a plan once he made it.

"Why would you need me, now or later?" Andreas

asked. "Your CEO would come to you for advice, surely, and you'll mentor your own children."

"I can give my children no greater gift than to assure they have access to good mentors in their lives."

Kayla didn't know about Andreas, but she was touched on his behalf.

He actually looked kind of gobsmacked. "That is quite an honor, but you know I planned to move on completely from KJ Software."

Kayla's heart sank at his confirmation of what she already knew.

"Yes, but would it really be such a burden to maintain nominal ownership in the company?"

And Kayla suddenly realized something. Sebastian Hawk really wanted this, had probably wanted it from the beginning of his negotiations with Andreas.

She looked at both men, realizing their arguments sounded almost rehearsed. Or rehashed. "You asked Andreas to stay on as nominal partner to begin with, but he refused."

"Despite his possessive attitude toward his business, he did." Andreas sounded disgruntled. "I let him know it was not an option."

"Things have changed, haven't they?" Sebastian prompted.

"Because I'm asking for something you *don't* want to give." Kayla didn't try to stifle her sigh of disappointment. Sebastian Hawk would rather have *her* as an employee than a business partner.

Kayla wasn't offended. She knew her strengths and they happened in the computer lab, not the conference room. That was undeniably Andreas's forte.

"Oh, I'm positive that under his cool demeanor, Hawk is thrilled you want to keep your ownership, *pethi mou.* He couldn't be sure you wouldn't be head-hunted otherwise."

Kayla looked between the men. Sebastian Hawk's expression gave nothing away. Andreas looked about as movable as a rock.

Things were not looking good for her.

"I can tell you that Andreas has not changed his mind about pulling out of KJ Software completely." Kayla's hope for a positive outcome to this meeting dwindled by the second. "I can also tell you that if you try to push me out of ownership of my company, I will walk away from it and I won't be signing any non-compete contracts either."

It wasn't a threat exactly. She knew she couldn't hope to compete with a company the size of Hawk Enterprises, but if he wasn't lying about truly valuing her expertise and creative programming ideas, he wanted to keep her on at KJ Software.

"You've trained her well, Andreas." Sebastian didn't sound annoyed. He did look just slightly amused.

Kayla could have cheerfully kicked his shin under the table. This was *her* life they were talking about.

Andreas must have read something on her face because he reached out and pulled her right hand out of its clasp with her left to hold it. "Stay calm, *pethi mou.* Hawk is a reasonable man."

"I have not refused and you are quite right, Kayla, your value to the company is such that I have no desire to see you move on. However, both of you must realize that KJ Software itself will do better with both Andreas and my expertise at its CEO's disposal. It's still a fairly new company and even folded into the structure of Hawk Enterprises, there are growing pains ahead."

Kayla agreed. Of course she did. If she had her way,

Andreas wouldn't be selling the company at all, but that wasn't what he wanted. He wanted to take his money and business skills and bring success to other ventures.

Andreas frowned. "Those growing pains will happen because it's a strong company that will add significantly to Hawk Enterprises."

"Agreed." Hawk didn't add anything else.

No compromise there. From either man.

"I came to New York to settle my future, not scuttle Andreas's plans." Kayla stood up. "I won't allow you to make my keeping my five percent a condition of the deal, Andreas. This is too important to you."

"And it is not important to you?" He stood too, his hand still holding hers. "Come, sit back down, this is part of business. I know not a part you enjoy, but that is why you needed me here."

She'd needed him there because he knew that Sebastian Hawk wanted something Kayla could never have promised on Andreas's behalf. Nor would she want to. She ignored his claim when she answered, "I think we've all said what needed saying."

She pulled her hand from his and turned to offer it to Sebastian. "Thank you for meeting with me. Let me know if you decide *my* terms are acceptable."

Sebastian had stood when Andreas did. He took her hand and shook it with all evidence of friendliness and good will. "Kayla, you are a brilliant programmer. Do not underestimate how much I want you to stay on at KJ Software."

Just not enough to make the deal without the added incentive of Andreas maintaining a connection to the company. She got the silent message.

Unable to force words past her suddenly constricted throat, she simply nodded.

Andreas cursed in Greek. It was something he did when he was really frustrated, a habit he'd developed young, he'd told her once. He'd learned the words from friends of his mother's, other transplanted Greeks she made sure he was exposed to during his childhood, wanting him to maintain a heritage from her homeland.

He moved quickly to stand beside her, his arm going around her waist in a way that was not at all appropriate for a business meeting. But then calling her by Greek endearments hadn't been either.

Andreas pulled her into his side. "Pleasure, Hawk. I put my own proposal forward to Kayla yesterday. If she agrees, you can consider your terms acceptable."

Kayla nearly choked on the air she was trying to drag into her lungs. He had not just said that. Peeking up at his profile, she was snagged by an all-too-serious green gaze.

She bit back her own epithet. Oh, he'd said it all right. And just like everything else he said, he meant it.

"Whatever you proposed must be very important to you." Sebastian was back to looking at her quizzically.

Kayla gave him a sickly smile. "Goodbye, Sebastian."

CHAPTER ELEVEN

Kayla followed Andreas into the suite. She'd maintained radio silence since his pronouncement at the restaurant, but there was plenty she wanted to say. Plenty.

Once the door closed behind them, she spun to face Andreas, but words actually failed her.

He shrugged out of his perfectly tailored jacket and even went so far as to tug off his tie before undoing a couple of buttons on his shirt.

"Well?" he prompted, when she just stood there in the center of the living area, her business suit wholly inadequate armor against the emotions he provoked in her.

"What do you mean, *well*? How could you say something like that?" Yes, her voice was a few decibels above normal and maybe she was waving her arms like a madwoman, but who would blame her?

"Something like what? Goodbye? Talk to you later?" he replied with totally inappropriate facetiousness.

"You know what! You told Sebastian Hawk you'd agree to his terms if I agreed to marry you."

Andreas shrugged, appearing supremely unconcerned. "Yes, I did."

"You don't want to keep any percent of the company."

Andreas undid another couple of buttons on his shirt.

"As Sebastian so astutely pointed out, your positive answer to my proposal is very important to me."

Now was not the time to notice how attractive the slice of hairy chest he revealed was.

"Enough to sell yourself?" she demanded, feeling like she was the one being sold.

"That is not how I see it." Andreas indicated she should sit on the plush cream sofa. Once she did, he lowered himself into the spot right beside her. "While you may dislike the negotiation side of things and find our methods cutthroat, I excel at them."

She knew that. She did. And having him on her side in negotiations was something powerful. "But using yourself in terms I know you can't want…"

"I knew what Sebastian would ask for before we went into that meeting. He's made no secret that he would prefer I maintain a nominal connection with the business since we started talks."

"When did you start those talks?" she couldn't help asking.

"Talks grew serious a couple of months ago." Andreas laid his arm across the back of the sofa, bringing his body that much closer to hers.

Which was enough of an answer. "I should have realized what you were up to. I knew your long-term plan," Kayla admitted to him and to herself.

Andreas only nodded in agreement, his expression serious and watchful.

"You consider my agreement to marry you important enough to keep that part of your assets tied up in the company?" she asked, still unable to believe that was the case.

"I do."

"Why?" He'd made it clear he did not love her.

He grimaced. Whether because he didn't want to answer the question or thought she should already know the answer, she didn't know. "Six years ago, I brought you into my business to keep you in my life."

In a way he understood and that he considered more permanent than the relationship they'd had at the time. She got that. Now.

"When you made me see that you would not be coming into my new company with me, I realized there had to be another answer to keeping the one person I consider family in my life in a significant way." He brushed her neck with his thumb, his expression oh, so serious.

"You never take time off," she observed.

His brows rose in mockery. "Pot? Meet kettle."

She smiled. "That's not what I mean. It's just, you came tearing after me when you realized I was in New York."

He'd reacted very badly to her being out of his sphere, almost panicked. She saw that now too.

"I hopped a plane, but your point is taken."

"Because I'm *that* important to you?"

"As I have said." His tone implied he didn't think he should have had to say so, then or now.

"But you don't love me."

"Is that a deal breaker for you?" he asked, rather than answer her.

She thought about it. Andreas would not let himself love her. And while that hurt, badly, she considered how it would impact their life together.

Sex between them was off the hook. They *were* best friends. Andreas got her in a way that no one else did. And she understood him in a way she hadn't before, in a way she knew no one else could.

But probably most importantly, she could not imagine her life without him in it. Oh, she was sure she could survive without the Greek tycoon, but honestly? She didn't want to. With every fiber of her being she did not want to build a life without Andreas Kostas in it.

"Kayla?" he prompted after her long silence.

"I had to think about it."

His other hand came to rest on her hip, surrounding her with his presence. "And?"

"No, it is not a deal breaker." She swallowed against a suddenly dry throat.

Green eyes flared with satisfaction and maybe just a little joy. "I am glad."

"You are not allowed to fall in love with anyone else either." She glared at him, letting him know she meant what she said. "I'm not marrying you only to be set aside later because you changed your mind about love."

His laughter was rich and very comforting. "That will not happen."

"We will adopt?"

"As soon as you like."

"But you want to try for a baby, as well."

"Melia Kostas's DNA deserves to live on to the next generation."

She laid her own hand against his chest, reveling in the warmth of his skin under his fitted dress shirt. "You know your father will consider the child his grand-child, as well."

"His arrogance would allow nothing less."

"Will you let our children have an extended family?" she asked, not sure the answer mattered to her decision, but curious all the same.

"So long as the Kostas and Georgas clans accept all of our children equally, yes."

"You didn't even have to think about that." She'd thought he would have a lot more trouble with the idea.

"Family is very important to you. Withholding myself and our children from my family would hurt you. I will not do that."

"You're really kind of amazing, you know that?"

"I'm very glad *you* think so."

"I'm not signing a prenup." Neither of them were going into this marriage with some kind of perfectly contracted-out clause.

His smile was wry. "Genevieve would have a coronary."

"She's no longer your bride pimp. You fired her."

"For good reason."

"Yes?" Kayla supposed Andreas would consider Genevieve's threat to come to New York in pursuit of him a good reason.

"She upset you."

"I thought you fired her because she threatened to come to New York."

"That was just the final straw, but you do not think I could have dealt with her desire to follow us here?"

Andreas could handle anything.

"I suppose." She smiled at him. "You can certainly handle your family now."

Which probably explained why he was willing to have the Georgas clan in his children's lives. Andreas was confident in his ability to protect *his* family from those who claimed the same status.

"Yes."

"Your dad let you go when you were eighteen. He didn't have to do that," she reminded him.

"He's a smart businessman. He's in the long game. Nothing else he had tried had worked to bring me into the fold. He believed that by supporting my desire to attend university in America, he might gain some favor with me finally."

"I'm not convinced that's all. After all, you changed your name back to Kostas, which was a slap in the face. He never threatened to remove your funding for school."

Andreas had told her that six years ago.

"No, but do not believe for one minute his arrogance was diminished in any way. He simply realized that my will in regard to who I am was greater than his."

She still thought there was more to it, but telling Andreas that his father loved him was going to go over like a lead balloon.

Love was not something Andreas Kostas wanted to consider as a motivation for life. But that didn't stop Kayla from being helplessly, hopelessly in love with him.

Maybe not so hopeless if he wanted to marry her.

He wasn't offering a love match, but he was offering his commitment, the kind of commitment that Andreas Kostas would never break. She really wasn't worried about him falling in love with someone else, because she knew that if he said he wouldn't look outside their marriage for companionship, he wouldn't.

His business took up far too much time and energy for him to have any left over for liaisons. And Kayla intended their home life to be everything Andreas dreamed of it being. Everything his mother had taught him to value.

"Okay, I'll marry you." She sighed and considered how deeply she loved this man. "And you do not have to make that deal with Sebastian for me to say *yes*. I would have regardless."

"As I explained to both of you, I will not entertain

a deal now that does not allow you to maintain a stake in the company."

"You could go public with the shares, hire a CEO to take over for you."

"That would not make the same guarantees for our employees that Sebastian has agreed to do."

Not unless Andreas kept a controlling interest. "You really have been trying to look out for everybody."

"As head shark, that is my job."

She laughed, but the sound was cut off by his lips. When the passionate kiss ended, she asked, "What are you doing?"

"Celebrating your answer in the best way I know how."

And they did.

The next morning, Kayla woke up next to the man of her dreams with the certain knowledge that he was hers. No matter why he wanted to marry her, they *were* going to wed and that meant a lifetime commitment for Andreas Kostas.

His handsome features were relaxed in sleep, the square jaw not too big-shark-businessman intimidating, his eyelashes sweeping under his eyes in peaceful repose. For once, he did not look ready to conquer the world, vulnerable in sleep just like any other man. Not that Andreas Kostas was average by any definition.

Larger-than-life, he'd been filling hers right up since they first met eight years ago on a university campus.

And now their lives would be joined. He wasn't interested in marrying a socialite or someone from an ancient family. Not even another shark, of the female variety. Andreas wanted to build a real family with Kayla.

Maybe some things *were* bigger than the concept of romantic love.

Green eyes opened, alert at once in a way she rarely woke up. "You are watching me in my sleep."

"That's usually your gig, I know."

He flashed her a very sexy smile. "It is so pleasurable to watch you when you're all soft and quiet."

She shook her head. "Crazy man."

"I assure you, I am as sane as the next man."

"Other men do not come off favorably when compared to you," she teased with the truth.

Andreas's gaze flashed emerald. "Good to know."

She sat up, pushing the sheet away. "I guess I'd better get packing."

"Why?" He gave her naked body an appreciative look filled with heat.

She stood, slipped her arms into his robe, knowing he wouldn't mind sharing, and walked toward the door of his bedroom, away from temptation. "Because I'm sure you've already told Bradley to arrange our flight."

"You know me well."

She looked around the luxurious suite's bedroom with something akin to sadness before meeting his eyes again. "I suppose my vacation is over."

"Who said?" Sitting up against the elegant fabric-covered headboard, he gave her a devil's grin. "Our flight isn't until the day after tomorrow."

"What? Why?" Her hand fell away from the door handle.

"I wanted a chance to do some more sightseeing with you."

"You? Sightseeing?" she asked, trying to understand this stranger looking so sexy in the bed. This was not Andreas as she knew him.

"We went the day before yesterday. You enjoyed yourself." His tone implied he thought that was all the explanation need.

She was still flummoxed. "I did."

"You are on vacation."

So she'd tried to convince him. "I thought you didn't believe in vacation."

His dark brows drew together in a frown. "I never said that."

"No, you've just spent the last six years without taking one." What else was she supposed to think? Even she had taken time off occasionally, especially when she'd finally been able to launch the shelter she'd always dreamed of.

"Well, I'm about to be married. Start a family. Vacation is something I will have to get used to."

She almost laughed at the way he said it, like taking a vacation was a painful condition he would have to learn to live with. "Time off to explore new places is supposed to be a good thing."

"Is that not what I'm saying?" The look of confusion on Andreas's face was cute, if a six-foot-four-inch business mogul could be called *cute*.

She guessed it was, as impossible as Kayla found that to believe. "Okay, sure. So, we have two more days?"

"I thought we could take a tour of Central Park today." He tilted his head, like he was trying to read her reaction. "It is said to be a highlight of visiting New York."

"You've been here several times for business, you never visited Central Park?" And he wanted to take her there?

"I had no reason to do so."

"But you do now?"

LUCY MONROE   185

"You will enjoy it."

She wasn't sure how to take that, other than to move back to the bed, climb over to him and lay her lips against his, her kiss filled with all the sense of joy and gratitude coursing through her. Happiness soon turned to passion, her body responding to his nakedness, her near nudity and his wondering hands.

It was a couple of hours before they were able to shower and sit down to breakfast.

Andreas had been right, the pedicab tour of Central Park was amazing, their driver a font of information about New York and the history of the park, his story-telling almost as mesmerizing as the way Andreas insisted on holding her hand and dropping random kisses on Kayla's temple, cheek and even lips. About halfway through the tour, their guide explained they'd need to walk up to the folly if they wanted to see Belvedere Castle firsthand, as no conveyances were allowed on the narrower path.

Keen to experience all that she could, Kayla looked up at Andreas. "Can we?"

"Definitely."

The trip up to Belvedere Castle was through a gorgeous English-style garden, worth the walk in itself, Kayla thought, and then said so.

"Agreed." Andreas stopped her in the middle of the garden area. "Are you going to want to sell our condos and buy a house, so we can have flowers?"

"A place for our children to play would be nice, but yes, I'd like flowers."

"Your collection of African violets on the window-sill in your condo gives you away."

She shrugged. "Plants make it more homey."

"Your presence always makes my condo feel more homey."

"You're awfully complimentary all of a sudden."

His expression went serious, his green gaze darkened with sincerity. "It is not sudden."

Unable to hold his gaze, and frankly uncomfortable with the conversation, Kayla made a show of examining the gardens. "This park really is amazing." She snapped a few shots with her camera phone. "So beautiful."

Andreas was looking at her, not the roses. "I know beautiful."

"Don't be silly."

"Speaking the truth is not foolish."

She rolled her eyes. "You really don't have to come over all complimentary now, Andreas. I've already agreed to marry you."

"When have I ever not thought you were beautiful?" he asked, obviously affronted. But giving her no chance to answer, he pulled her into his arms and kissed her.

Deeply. No affectionate peck like while riding in the pedicab was this one. He laid claim to her again with his lips, right there, in front of the other tourists and park visitors.

She found herself responding, and as uncaring of their audience as he obviously was, she buried her hands in his perfect businessman's haircut, tugging at his hair in her ardor.

After several pleasurable moments, he groaned and set her away from him. "We must stop, *pethi mou*, or there will be no continuing this excursion."

She reached up and patted down the tufts of hair her wandering fingers had caused. "Okay, but you owe me."

"A debt I will always enjoy paying." He took her

hand. "We'd better get going. The pedicab driver is waiting on us."

She nodded.

They were at the folly, when Andreas spoke again, his words surprising her. "When my father came to get me, he gave me no time to pack, telling me he would provide anything I needed."

"I know he forced you to go with him, but didn't he have his minions pack up you and your mom's apartment?"

"He might have given me a chance to pack my own things, but I was so resistant to going to Greece with him that his bodyguards had to force me into the car and the airplane after that. He disposed of almost everything, believing I needed nothing from my previous life in America."

"Your dad is a real 'bull in the china shop' kinda guy, isn't he?" And the man's ways were guaranteed to drive wedges between Barnabas Georgas and his only, very strong-willed, son.

"Yes. He does not consider his actions in light of the feelings of others."

"Maybe no family is better than that kind of family."

Andreas surprised her by shaking his head. "No. He will be an adequate grandfather and our future children deserve to know where they come from."

"Are you sure?"

"I am." Andreas sighed as they climbed the stairs to the turret in the folly. "My father's proclivity for bullish action is not what I wanted to talk about."

"It's not?"

"No. As I said, he threw out everything of my mother's, but he did have his bodyguards pack up some minimal clothes for me, until such time as he could replace them, and my box of mementos because if a boy my age kept one, clearly what was inside was treasured."

"He told you that?"

Andreas pulled her into a surprisingly deserted overlook. "He did."

So, not a complete monster, but she knew all too well how devastating it was to be uprooted and lose everything familiar. It had happened to her often enough in foster care, and it had not gotten any easier with the repetition.

"And?" She really didn't know where this was going.

Andreas pulled a small velvet bag out of his pocket and gave it to her.

"What is this?" she asked, even as she loosened the drawstring to pull out a delicate silver chain.

On the end was what looked like an antique pendant, a silver oval locket about twice the size of a quarter. The front was etched with a fine filigree, a Greek cursive *K* worked into the center.

"It's gorgeous."

"My mother always thought so."

"This was hers?" Kayla asked in wonder.

"It was in my box of keepsakes, the only piece of her jewelry not disposed of by my father."

"I'm sorry," Kayla said, sharing his pain.

"I was too, but the other pieces weren't valuable."

"Still, they were hers."

"Yes." He reached up and brushed Kayla's cheek. "You may look inside if you like."

She wasted no time opening the locket. Inside was a miniature formal shot of a young boy, maybe ten years old, his eyes and jawline very familiar.

Kayla smiled at the precious image, and the one of

the beautiful woman in the opposite oval. "Was this you, and your mom?"

"Yes. The locket is now yours, to do with what you will." His expression was hard to read, almost like he was waiting for her to reject the gift.

Touched beyond anything, she choked out, "It looks old."

"It has been handed down through many generations of Kostas. Traditionally, it was given to the eldest son for his wife, but my father gave it to my mother when they disowned her."

"Compensation for losing her family?" Kayla asked in disbelief.

"My mother said it was a reminder that while they could not acknowledge me, or her, if she insisted on keeping me, they still *loved* her." Oh, the cynicism he infused that word with.

"You said the family depended on the Georgas empire for their livelihood."

Andreas shrugged, dismissing that consideration. "They could have moved, found another place to work. Anything but give up their daughter for the sake of expediency."

"You would never do that."

"No. My children will know that they come before business concerns, or the approval of others."

"She kept it, the locket. It was important to her. And then she gave it to you?"

"Just before she died, yes." Andreas's jaw tightened. "She treasured it, just as she treasured the letters her mother wrote her, despite the fact my grandmother refused to buck tradition and have a public relationship with her disgraced daughter."

"The only disgrace was the way her family treated her." Of that Kayla had no doubts.

Melia Kostas had been an amazing person, not the kind of mom to abandon her three-year-old child at a truck stop. Kayla was glad Andreas had had that kind of mom, at least until he was fourteen.

He leaned down and kissed Kayla's temple, like he was saying thank you for her words. "I agree."

"But you still treasure this heirloom" She could see it in the way Andreas looked at the locket dangling from her fingers.

"Very much. It is the only thing I have that belonged to my mother, but it is also an opportunity to continue a Kostas tradition, only make it my own. That was important to Mama."

"And you're giving it to me?" To do with as she pleased. He'd said so, but the only thing she could imagine doing with the necklace was keeping it.

"I am. One day, you will pass it on to our oldest child."

So, he assumed she would continue the tradition, but she found the expectation made her happy, not stifled. "Oldest *born* child?" she clarified.

"No. The oldest child we bring into our family, boy or girl. My son or daughter will know that traditions connect us to past generations, but we are not bound by them."

Emotion choked Kayla's throat even tighter. "You are going to be a wonderful dad."

"I strive to excel." Another man might be joking when he said something like that, but she knew Andreas wasn't.

A wave of love for this incredible man washed over her, the necklace in her hand giving her a tiny spark of hope that their upcoming marriage would not be as lacking in emotion on his side as he claimed. The man wanted to give her a part of the one person in the world he'd ever admitted loving.

"Put it on me?" she asked.

Andreas's gaze darkened with some unnamed emotion. "By all means."

After doing the clasp, he brushed his lips against her nape. "There. Perfect."

Kayla spent the rest of their tour in a happy daze, the weight of the locket a constant reminder that Andreas valued her on a level he did not anyone else. Was that love?

Could the emotion exist without the words?

CHAPTER TWELVE

AFTER ANOTHER INCREDIBLE night of sightseeing, followed by a romantic dinner and lovemaking that lasted into the wee hours, Kayla got to sit next to Andreas in first class for their flight home.

He was solicitous, but then that wasn't exactly new. However, Kayla saw his actions through new eyes. When he ordered her favorite drink, when it became clear he'd called ahead for a special dinner prep for them, when Andreas offered to play cards rather than losing himself in work during the five-and-a-half-hour flight, she felt cherished.

Kayla also recognized he would have done those things for her, had in fact in the past, even if they had not become lovers again. She knew he wasn't that caring with his girlfriends, or anyone else. Full stop.

She didn't want to dwell on what it might mean. Six years ago, she'd believed he loved her despite the lack of words. Had even thought he would propose when he told her he had a proposition for her. When it turned out he wanted her to join him on his upcoming business venture, but in order for them to work together they had to stop having sex—and he'd put it just like that—Kayla's heart had broken. And she'd learned to doubt her own intuitive sense about people.

Yet she couldn't help feeling like there was more to her and Andreas in the emotional arena than he was willing to admit, was even beginning to wonder if there always had been.

The following weeks fell into a pattern. Kayla spent the day working, but Andreas was always there at the end of the day to take her home, or out to dinner, to a play or a performance at one of the theaters in downtown Portland. After which she would return to his condominium with him, where they'd plan a surprisingly big, formal wedding, as well as going over the houses—what Kayla privately considered mansions—the property broker had found for them to look at, and always, always, *always* end up making love before sleeping together in Andreas's bed.

"What's the rush with the wedding?" Kayla asked one morning after a fun but exhausting evening of tastings at the caterer's and wedding cake samplings.

Andreas adjusted his tie in the mirror, his bespoke suit immaculate. "You know that once I've made up my mind, I prefer to act."

Kayla slipped into her shoes. "You do realize most people take a year or more to plan a wedding of this magnitude?"

"Our guest list is not that large."

She made a scoffing sound. "In whose universe?"

Andreas had surprised her by agreeing to invite both sides of his family from Greece on her request. However, he'd also insisted on inviting friends like Sebastian Hawk and his wife, and *all* of the KJ Software employees.

"Would you have rather eloped?" He turned from the mirror and faced her, his hand coming to rest on her waist at it so often did.

If they were in the same room, he was touching her. If he was working in his office and she was in her lab, he texted or called. He was seducing her heart as surely as he did her body.

"No." She liked the idea of having witnesses to their vows, people who would share the memory of she and Andreas promising a lifetime together.

"So, we invite everyone."

"I still don't know how the wedding planner found a venue, caterers, a top-notch photographer and even a pastry chef for the cake on such short notice." Didn't it usually take several months ahead of time to order a huge formal wedding cake from the kind of bakery they'd engaged?

"I only hire the best, as you well know."

Kayla shook her head. "Giving her only two months was insane." They were a month out from the wedding, and while the last one had been the happiest of Kayla's life, it had also been nuts with planning.

"And yet she came through," Andreas said smugly. No one would claim Andreas Kostas was humble.

Good thing she *liked* his arrogance.

"Only because you were willing to pay such a premium for everything." Kayla shook her head. "It's ridiculous how much you're spending on this wedding."

"Not to me. The world will know I take this marriage seriously."

Her heart warmed at his words, further confirmation that despite the fact he still maintained his attitude that love was a weakness, his regard for her was well beyond what it was for anyone else.

"But then why do we have to find a house right now too?" she almost whined, thinking of the multiple viewings they had set up for that evening after work with a property broker. It was sort of her fault there were more than a couple, but she wasn't settling into some mansion that didn't feel like a home to raise children. "Don't you want to stay in and just relax for one night?"

Andreas pulled her body flush with his. "I want you living with me."

"So, I'll move in here officially." Talking was losing its appeal, but if she gave in and kissed him, they'd be late for work. Not something that would help either of their schedules. "I spend all my time here anyway."

"It is a waste of time and resources to move you twice." The shrug in his voice couldn't be more pronounced.

"Says you." Most of her clothes had already migrated to his closet, but she still had to go to her condo daily to water her plants, sort her mail, etc. She frowned up at him. "So, we are going to rush into buying a house?"

"Only if we find one we both like." He leaned down and kissed her chastely, though the touch sparked very unchaste desires in her.

Kayla shook her head again, as much to clear it as to let him know she wasn't buying it. "All of the houses we're going to look at tonight are amazing."

"So, presumably it will be no difficulty to choose one for us to begin our family in."

"I still don't understand why everything has to happen this minute." Yes, he was the kind of guy who acted after making a decision, but the pace of these changes in their lives was overwhelming.

"I want you settled in my life."

She laid her forehead against his chest, just enjoying the connection for a second. "I'm already in your life, Andreas, if you hadn't noticed."

"I noticed."

"So?" She looked up at him again, wanting to see his face.

The vulnerability she found there left Kayla breathless.

Andreas's mouth firmed. "I want the ties."

Again her heart filled, nearly to bursting, at the evidence of how much he wanted to cement her place with him. "You make it difficult to stay irritated with you, Dre."

"That is a good thing."

Kayla wasn't feeling so charitable a couple of days later as she headed toward Andreas's office for a surprise meeting. The last one hadn't gone so well for her. Bradley had been really cagey when he'd called to tell her Andreas needed her in his office at three o'clock too. Kayla couldn't help but worry. She wasn't sure what she thought her new fiancé was up to, but whatever it was, Kayla was not ready for one more change in her life.

Bradley waved her through when she got to Andreas's office suite, a strange expression on the PA's face.

"What is this about?" Kayla demanded, stopping at Bradley's desk.

"I can't say."

"That doesn't mean you don't know."

"Just go in, Kayla. Please."

Her heart in her toes, sure Andreas had found the CEO to take over for him already, Kayla did as Bradley asked. She wasn't ready for Andreas not to be working at KJ Software yet. Not that he'd leave immediately, she knew that. He'd have to train his replacement, but still, it was the beginning of the end.

The woman sitting on a leather sofa—*not* at the conference table—that was part of the conversational group by the window looked far too young and frankly *soft* to be a corporate-shark CEO. Dressed in a trendy top and calf-length skinny slacks, the woman was Kayla's age, if not a couple of years younger. Her clothes were stylish, but not corporate sharp or expensive designer label.

There was something familiar about the gray eyes that had locked on to Kayla the moment she walked into the office, though. The woman with delicate features and golden-brown hair, just this side of blonde, gasped and then her eyes filled with moisture.

Kayla did not understand what was happening. She looked to her fiancé and demanded, "Andreas?"

He came toward her quickly, laying a possessive arm around her waist as he guided her toward the sofa and chairs. "Kayla, *pethi mou*, I would like you to meet your sister."

Kayla's knees gave way, her joints and muscles turned to water in her shock. It was only Andreas's arm around her that stopped Kayla from collapsing to the floor.

"My sister?" she asked, her voice barely above a whisper, her heart beating so fast, she thought she might pass out.

Andreas's hold on her tightened as he guided her to a chair catty-corner from where the other woman was sitting.

"Yes," both Andreas and the woman said at the same time.

The woman, Kayla's sister…her *sister*, leaned toward her, gray eyes so familiar because they were just like Kayla's, she now realized, filled with what looked like hope. "I didn't know I had a sister."

"Then how? No, wait, what's your name?" Kayla needed that piece of information.

Andreas made a noise that would have indicated embarrassment in anyone else. "I should have said."

"I go by Miranda Smith now, but my friends call me Randi."

"Go by…now… What does that mean?"

"She had reason to change her name as a teenager," Andreas offered.

"Because of our mom?" Kayla realized it was just as possible they shared a father.

Randi's mouth twisted with disgust. "No. That particular issue had nothing to do with the crazy woman who gave us birth."

"Our mom is mentally ill." Kayla wasn't sure how she felt about her sister using the *crazy* word.

"That's what her defense attorney claimed after she tried to drown me in the bathtub at age six. However, I do not believe that a terrible temper mixed with drug abuse is in and of itself a mental illness."

"She tried to kill you?" Kayla asked in pained disbelief.

Randi grimaced. "I'm not sure abandoning a three-year-old at a truck stop is any better."

"But someone found me and turned me in to the authorities." According to her records, Kayla hadn't been in the best condition when she was turned over to child services, but she could not remember if that was due to her mom or the time between the abandonment and her being rescued.

"She didn't care what happened. That's the point. She never cares about anyone else. I'm sorry. I know it hurts to hear, but our mom's life has always been about what she wants, about her comfort. No one else has ever mattered enough for her to change her behavior. They do say narcissism is a diagnosable psychological condition. I'll give her that one."

Kayla could feel Randi's pain and knew with certainty that life with their mom had been awful, the attempted drowning only one terrible memory.

Kayla looked up at Andreas before meeting her sister's gray gaze again. "I guess foster care wasn't so bad after all."

Randi made a pained sound. "You should never have been raised by strangers. You had a family that selfish bitch stole from you. Our grandparents are amazing. My dad would have accepted you as his own. Marla took away all our choices when she abandoned you."

"You sound very bitter."

"I do, don't I?" Randi's smile was warm, genuine and big. "I'm not. Really. I may despise our mother, but my dad didn't allow her to terrorize my entire childhood. He really is a great guy and like I said, Mom's parents are pretty wonderful. They and my dad's parents always stood by me."

"But you changed your name?" There was a story there.

"It was necessary for me to become more anonymous."

Something really bad had happened and Kayla couldn't help feeling her sister might have had the more difficult life, despite having a family. She hoped someday Randi would feel good about confiding in her, but right now, she was just so happy she had a sister.

"So, you're saying you were happy despite our mom?" Kayla asked with a smile of her own.

"Yeah. I just wish you'd been part of my growing up." There was no doubting the sincerity of the other woman.

"How old are you?"

"Twenty-four."

So, four years younger than Kayla. "You were born the year after she abandoned me."

"She moved back to live with our grandparents. She met my dad at their church. She was pretending to be the perfect daughter."

"And an illegitimate daughter wouldn't have fit into that image." That knowledge should have hurt, but it wasn't far off from things she'd already thought.

"Grandma and Grandpa wouldn't have cared about that. They would have loved you, would like a chance to love you now, but Mom, she thought she'd do better coming home to them without a child."

"But…"

"Look, sometimes the apple falls so far from the tree, it lands in a different state. That was our mom and our grandparents."

Kayla believed Randi, her usual distrust of new people conspicuously absent. Still, it was overwhelming. "I don't know what to say."

"Say you'll give me a chance to know you. Look, I know I'm going about some of this wrong." Randi gave Kayla a self-deprecating smile. "I feel like all my training flew out the window when you walked in here, but you're my sister and we deserve to have that bond."

"Your training?" Kayla asked, feeling lost. Again.

"I have a degree in social work. It's what I do, work with abandoned and abused kids, trying to help them have better lives."

"Wow." Kayla and this woman really were sisters. "You turned your bad into good."

"I tried. I'm sorry if my honesty made me sound

bitter and broken. I'm not really, I just don't want you taken in by our mom."

"You're trying to protect me?"

"That's my job. We're sisters."

"You think that now you know about me our mom will find me?" How?

"If she does, and she finds out how well you've done for yourself, I guarantee she'll show up on your doorstop with a sob story and her hand out."

"I've had her investigated," Andreas inserted. "Your sister is quite right. We don't want that woman in our lives."

Kayla nodded, believing him. Maybe someone else would crave meeting their mother, regardless of who she was and what she was like, but that wasn't Kayla. She'd never looked for her mom because the idea of a woman capable of abandoning Kayla the way she had never seemed like someone she wanted to meet.

"You just confirmed what I always suspected," Kayla assured both Randi and Andreas.

"So, how did you find Randi?" Kayla asked Andreas. "Why did you go looking?"

"I hired an investigator. Your sister's ancestry hobby gave us the break we needed. Matching DNA." He smiled at Randi. "As to the why? Family is important to you, Kayla. If I could provide your own for you, nothing would stop me from doing so."

"And if you'd only found Marla?" Randi asked.

"You would never know I had even looked," Andreas said to Kayla.

Kayla had no trouble believing that claim, nor did she think he was wrong.

"How long are you here for?" Kayla asked Randi.

"I fly home on the red-eye. Getting time off from

work last minute wasn't easy and I couldn't take extra days."

That was when Kayla learned Miranda and the rest of her family were from California. Kayla took the remainder of the afternoon off to spend with her sister, both frightened and relieved when Andreas insisted on her taking time alone with Randi, to get to know her. They spent hours together, chatting while they walked the Rose Gardens, played at OMSI and had dinner at a yummy Italian restaurant downtown.

She dropped Randi off at the airport, and was still sniffling and trying to stifle her tears when she walked into Andreas's condo hours later.

He was working on his laptop, but stood up the moment she walked in. "How did it go?"

"We're so alike, we even have the same favorite Italian dish."

"She seemed like a very nice person from the investigator's report." He tugged her toward the sofa, where he sat them both down and put his arm around her. "And finding out about your mom? How are you doing with that?"

"I prefer to think of her as the egg donor."

His lips tilted in a half smile. "All right, the egg donor, then."

"It's kind of the fulfillment of all my nightmares in that regard. I thought, hey, maybe she just didn't love me, but to find out she could try to kill her own child, that she's manipulative and cruel." Kayla offered honesty she never would have before, even with Andreas. "It makes me nauseated to know I'm related to her. Like what if that kind of badness lives inside me?"

"No, you are kind and good, the best woman I know."

"Really? But—"

He wouldn't let her finish. "Don't you dare disparage yourself. You are not only the product of that woman's genes. Somewhere out there is a sperm donor, as well."

Kayla laughed a little at Andreas using a twist on her term for her missing father.

"You heard your sister. Your grandparents are good, kind people. Their daughter is nothing like them and you are nothing like her." Andreas's voice rang with sincerity and almost a desperate need for her to believe him.

"You're sure?"

"I'm positive."

She cuddled in closer to the man she loved. "Thank you. For everything."

"You are welcome."

"I don't know how to show just how much it means to me that you found my sister." And that he'd helped her deal with the reality of who her egg donor was.

His attitude helped her to see that she could move on from the past that she would not allow to define her. Andreas believed in her; he always had. And that mattered so much.

Andreas grin was sensual and mischievous. "I can think of a way."

Kayla laughed through her emotional tears, but she was only too happy to show him her gratitude with her body. The pleasure was so completely mutual. And she loved the power she felt when she had his sex in her mouth. He refused to climax that way, though, wanting to be inside her and bring her to her own orgasm before he was willing to come himself.

She was lying in the circle of his arms, satiated, her heart so full, there were only three words she could speak right then. No matter what he said he felt, or did not feel, he deserved to know what she did.

She curled into his side and whispered against his skin, "I love you, Andreas. Completely and forever. I have since the beginning."

His arms tightened around her, his body rolling toward hers. "Thank you."

She peeked up at him. He looked happy. There was no other description for the expression on his face, the glow in his green eyes.

"I will treasure your feelings for the gift they are." He leaned down and kissed her to seal his words, the action tender and perfect.

She didn't ask if he reciprocated. Clearly, he still wasn't ready to admit to feelings he considered a weakness, but he respected hers. And that was all she needed.

For now.

Randi flew in the week before the wedding, insisting that was what sisters did. Kayla had never had real family, so she couldn't say, but she liked having someone there to help her talk Andreas off the ledge when the caterers wanted to make a last-minute change to the menu.

"That dress is even more beautiful in person than it was on the video call." Randi smiled in sisterly approval at Kayla.

Kayla gave herself a critical appraisal in the full-size three-paneled mirror provided in the bridal preparation suite at their venue. The winter-white satin-and-chiffon strapless dress had been created by a local who had been a finalist on that reality show about upcoming clothing designers. The skirt fell in layers of chiffon, a cascade of Kayla's signature peach peeking out from the frothy folds.

She'd found a pair of two-inch heels with delicate cross straps that could be died to match the peach exactly. Her hair and makeup had been done by professionals, Andreas had insisted.

"I feel like a princess." Trite, she knew, but true. Kayla had never felt so lovely.

"Every bride should on her wedding day." Miranda gave her a one-armed hug, careful not to crush the beautiful dress. "So, you're glad you gave in about the stylist and her crew?"

Kayla sighed. "Yes. I didn't realize how different I would feel."

"I hope I marry a guy who cares about the details to make me feel special like your fiancé."

"I hope you find a man you love as much as I do Andreas." Kayla said nothing about the lack of love on Andreas's side. She didn't think a man could make his bride feel more cherished and cared for than Andreas had done for her.

Kayla went to put on the simple diamond studs Andreas had gifted her for Christmas four years previous. A rather personal gift for his employee/business partner, but Andreas made his own rules about life.

Miranda held out an elegant black box tied with a white bow before Kayla could put the earrings on. "Andreas told me to give this to you this morning."

Surprised, Kayla took the gift. "What is it?"

"I don't know." Miranda grinned. "But I'm guessing jewelry."

Kayla's sister was right. Inside the box, she found a pair of teardrop pearl earrings, matching necklace and bracelet. The tops of the earrings were a cluster of diamonds, the necklace falling to a gorgeous swirl of diamonds, a single pearl in the center, the bracelet a triple strand of interspersed pearls and diamonds, all the pearls in the jewelry the same soft peach of her dress and shoes. "How did he know?"

Miranda shrugged. "He knows *you*? I mean what were the chances your wedding dress wasn't going to have your color in it? But even if you'd gone fully traditional, the jewelry would have complemented it and allowed you to wear your signature color."

"He can be really thoughtful."

"I'd say that man spends a lot of time thinking about what is going to make you happy."

"You think so?"

"Don't you?" Miranda asked, a small frown marring her pretty features.

Kayla nodded. "Yes, I do. It's just, he's not big on the words, you know?"

"You know what they say? Actions speak louder than words."

Kayla was really beginning to believe they did. She finished putting on the jewelry, leaving off the necklace and wearing the locket he'd given her in New York instead, just before the wedding planner came in to give her the five-minute warning.

The wedding went by in a blur, the promises Kayla and Andreas spoke wrapping her in a fog of happiness she floated on going into the reception. She wasn't surprised that all of Andreas's family he'd invited had come. Nor did it shock her that so many of their employees had shown up, as well as the few external friends-cum-business-associates. Even on short notice.

No, the sheer numbers did not surprise Kayla, but they did overwhelm her. Her emotions swirled inside her, with no real outlet. For the first time in her life, she had family. She'd met her grandparents and Miranda's dad, who assured her they *were* family too, all of whom sat in the front row across the aisle from Andreas's father, his wife and grandparents from both sides of his Greek family.

She realized their employees made up the biggest portion of the guests, but knowing all these people had come to see her and Andreas make a lifetime commitment left her feeling both blessed and raw inside. Exposed in a way she'd worked very hard not to be since her years in the foster care system.

Andreas seemed to be in his element, distant but cordial with all of his guests, even Barnabas Georgas.

It was Kayla who felt like the buffer of her newfound happiness wasn't enough. Despite knowing they all wished her and Andreas well, or she assumed they did, she found being the center of attention wearing and even conversing with her newly discovered family was making her want to hide, rather than be the center of all this attention.

Knowing the wedding planner wanted her and Andreas to cut the cake, Kayla slipped behind a cluster of pots holding live plants taller than she was. She just needed a minute to breathe.

She'd been there only a couple of minutes when she heard a spate of Greek in an older man's voice, just on the other side of the green foliage.

"Speak English if you expect me to answer you," Andreas replied in a cold tone, his veneer of cordiality gone.

"You had to choose a nobody to marry?" Barnabas Georgas replied, his Greek accent faint, sounding more English than American.

"Kayla is somebody. She is my wife. I don't need you to approve of her. I have nothing to prove to you."

Andreas's tone was firm, but underlined with a sense of wonder.

Kayla felt tears prickle her eyes. He'd finally figured it out. He didn't have to show the Georgas or Kostas clans *anything*. Andreas did not need their respect or approval. Now he seemed to realize that.

"She has no family!" Barnabas Georgas was stuck on his theme, ignorant of Andreas's amazing breakthrough.

"On the contrary, her grandparents and her sister are here. I introduced you, or did you forget?" The snide implication could not be missed.

"I did not forget, but I had her investigated. She grew up in foster care, she has no real connections. I must assume her sister and grandparents are only making themselves known because she's marrying a very wealthy man."

Kayla sucked in air, the pain of the accusation acute.

CHAPTER THIRTEEN

"You know what they say about assumptions," Andreas drawled. "Only in this case, the only ass I see is you."

"Andreas!" Mr. Georgas did not like being criticized.

But Kayla loved the way Andreas's words made *her* feel. He was standing up for her. It wasn't a surprise, but it did wave that flicker of hope into a bright flame.

"What, Barnabas? You think you can question the motives of my wife's family when you know nothing of them?" Andreas demanded, his tone colder than Antarctica's windchill factor. "You think you can put down the woman I have chosen to spend the rest of my life with and I will tolerate it? She is what is important here. Not you. Not your approval."

Oh, how Andreas's words seized Kayla's heart.

"You could have married an heiress, a proper Greek girl."

Kayla shook her head. Yeah, that was never going to happen.

"Like your wife?" Andreas asked, his tone dangerous if his father only realized it.

Kayla moved some foliage aside so she could see the two men talking, eavesdropping without shame.

"Yes, like Hera."

"The woman you married, but not the woman who gave you a son," Andreas pointed out brutally.

Mr. Georgas's face twisted with pain for a brief moment, then he scowled at his son. "Yes. Even if I had not been married when we met, I would never have married Melia. You need to accept that and move on."

"Why? Because she was a mere employee? Because she had no money or connections to bring to the table?" Andreas's tone made it clear what he thought of his father's reasoning, and it wasn't complimentary.

"Precisely. I needed a wife who could handle entertaining for my business, who would not embarrass me."

The sound Andreas made was worse than disgust, it was utter contempt. "Melia Kostas could not have embarrassed you. She had integrity, goodness and kindness."

"But no breeding, like the woman you chose to marry, out of spite for me I have no doubt."

Hearing the words from Barnabas Georgas's mouth made Kayla realize how silly her own thoughts in that arena had been. Didn't the man realize that Andreas did not think like that?

Andreas threw his gorgeous head back and laughed. "Do not give yourself so much credit!"

Kayla felt a smile curve her lips.

"Where is your bride right now?" Mr. Georgas asked with judgment. "She is not mingling with the guests, making connections on your behalf as Hera has done for me time and again. I noted how out of her depth she was, you had to see it too."

"What the hell are you talking about?" Andreas didn't sound angry, he sounded worried.

And Kayla knew he wasn't thinking about the networking she wasn't using her wedding reception to do.

He was worried about *her* because his father brought up that he thought Kayla felt out of her depth.

"Your new wife hates being the center of attention," Georgas said with disdain. "She could not be bothered to greet me, or the rest of your family."

"I hadn't yet made the time to introduce you." And Andreas didn't sound like he felt badly about that either.

His father rolled his eyes. "She's a liability."

"You can say that when she's the *only* reason you, or any of my Greek connections, were invited today?"

"We are not connections, we are your family."

"Which is why *she* wanted me to mend fences." His emphasis on *she* wasn't lost on the older man, who grimaced. Andreas stepped back from his father, creating more than physical distance between them. "She believes our children should have an extended family, but you'll have nothing to do with them, or me, if you can't show Kayla the respect she deserves."

"She's pregnant?" Mr. Georgas asked almost eagerly, and like suddenly he understood.

"No, she's not pregnant." Andreas got a look in his eye that Kayla knew well. "In fact, we do hope to adopt soon, though."

"Adopt?"

"Yes, adopt." Andreas met his father's gaze, his own stony green. "Our children will know only acceptance, however they come to be part of our family."

"I accepted you. You never accepted your Greek family."

"My mother was Greek. I accepted her. She gave me life, but more importantly, she fought and worked so hard to give me a life worth having. She never considered my birth an inconvenience. She did not need me to be a success, or groomed, to approve of and love me."

Oh, Andreas was having all sorts of insights and breakthroughs. Kayla blinked back tears of joy as she realized the man she loved was breaking the fetters of painful bonds that had held him for years.

"That is not how I saw it!"

"So, why offer her money to get rid of me?" Andreas almost sounded like he didn't care about the answer.

Kayla knew better.

Mr. Georgas harrumphed. "I was married. You're old enough to understand the world is not roses and rainbows."

"I'm old enough to understand that some men are weak and some women are strong. You guess which category you belong in."

Oh, harsh! Kayla brought her hand over her mouth.

Mr. Georgas turned red, opened his mouth, no doubt to blast Andreas, but Kayla wasn't going to let that happen.

"This conversation is devolving fast." Kayla forced herself to speak, coming from around the ficus tree. She looked to Mr. Georgas. "Do you want to be allowed into Andreas's life?"

The older Greek man made a visible effort to collect himself. "I do."

"Even if that means accepting his marriage to a woman you don't consider good enough for him?" Kayla didn't care if the man approved of her, especially knowing how much that *didn't* matter to the man she had married.

"Yes," Mr. Georgas said, no waffling in his tone or manner.

"You are more than good enough for me, *pethi mou*, you are the *best* for me!" Andreas was still glaring at his father with too much venom.

Kayla smiled up at him, reaching out to brush a finger along his jawline. "It makes me really happy you think so, but Mr. Georgas is right about some things. I'm never going to be a social butterfly. This wedding and reception *have been* really overwhelming for me."

Andreas took both her hands in his, staring down at her like she was the only person in the room. "I'm sorry. I should have realized. He shouldn't have had to point it out to me."

"That is all you got from what I said?" his father asked with disgust.

"That is all that matters," Andreas said. "She's mine. And I take care of what's mine."

"You're so possessive." Kayla couldn't help the smile she gave her husband. "I like it."

"You two are ridiculous."

Kayla met Mr. Georgas's eyes while moving to stand in the circle of Andreas's arms. "We are happy. I think if you'd just stop sniping at him, you'd find some happiness in your relationship with your son too."

"How dare you speak to me that way?"

"Because I'm the one person who has full access. I'm the one person Andreas will change his mind, his plans and his intentions to make happy. Do you really think it's in your best interests to keep putting me down? He's not going to divorce me and marry some woman you find more suitable."

"You're awfully confident for a woman he broke up with once already," the Greek man blustered.

"That was before."

"Before what?"

"Before he realized he loved me."

Andreas sucked in a breath, his hold on her tightening with near-painful intensity. "You believe I love you?"

She smiled up at him, really at peace for the first time that day so that her newfound joy made her near incandescent with it. "I know you do."

"He's never said the words?" Mr. Georgas asked, subdued instead of snarky.

So, Kayla didn't take offense. "He doesn't need to. Everything he does is about keeping me in his life."

"And you believe that means he loves you?"

"I know it does." Kayla sighed. "Look, I get that you and Andreas don't have a great relationship, but what you need to understand is that won't change if you keep up this bullish attitude. For my sake, he invited you to our wedding. Don't pour your own guilt and self-recrimination all over that like fertilizer. Nothing good is going to grow from it, I promise."

"You are a very blunt woman."

Kayla shrugged. Socially inept. Blunt. Lost in her own world. She could be all those things, but they didn't bother Andreas. He was the one who really mattered. And she'd discovered what others might consider her shortcomings didn't seem to bother her sister in the slightest either. What more did Kayla need?

Not this man's approval. But he needed hers if he wanted to be a grandfather someday. "We are going to adopt. That is a given. One day, we may have biological children, as well." Sooner than later if she didn't get on some birth control, but she wasn't going to mention that. "What you need to decide is if you can accept me, our children—all of them—or not?"

"And if I don't, Andreas will finally cut me off completely. That is what you are saying."

"Not Kayla, me." Andreas leaned down and kissed the top of Kayla's fancy updo. "She's the only reason

I'm giving you any kind of chance now. What you do with that chance is up to you."

"Family is important."

"When family isn't toxic, I would agree." Oh, Andreas was not giving an inch.

Mr. Georgas finally seemed to realize that. "You are my son, though you refuse to carry my name." His lips twisted in frustration, but he went on. "I will congratulate you on your marriage as I should have done to begin with. Kayla is right, my own guilt and old pains were at the root of my criticisms."

It was clear the admission cost the older man.

Andreas inclined his head. "We accept your congratulations, but be aware, there will be no second chances when it comes to *any* of our children."

"I believe you." Mr. Georgas let out a long breath. "You've done well for yourself, Andreas."

"Without the Georgas name or money to back me."

Kayla elbowed Andreas, but he acted like he didn't feel it.

"I know you don't believe it, but I love Hera and always have done. My time with your mother was an aberration and I took out my own guilt on her, as well. We knew Hera couldn't have children. Accepting you, or even supporting her having you, seemed like a worse betrayal to my wife than the affair. She'd had three miscarriages. Hera was lost in a sea of misery when I turned to Melia for comfort."

"My mother was a good woman."

"Yes, she was. She was a better person than me at the time. Do you know she never asked me to leave Hera? Even when Melia realized she was pregnant, she did not want to break up my marriage. I believe she loved me, but she knew I did not love her."

"She sounds like an amazing and, yes, a very strong woman," Kayla said.

"She was," both father and son said together.

Kayla smiled. "So, you're sorry you asked Melia to get rid of the baby, aren't you?"

"I am." Mr. Georgas's eyes glistened, his face showing so much pain. "If I could take the words back and never have spoken them, I would."

"Because you want an heir," Andreas said, anger absent from his voice, but no softness there either.

"Because you are my son and I love you." Mr. Georgas let out a deep breath.

"It sounds to me like you had the genuine love of two very special women in your life," Kayla pointed out. "Hera clearly forgave you for the affair."

"She did. She is and, yes, Melia was, as well."

"Why try so hard to erase her from my life, then?" Andreas demanded.

"Because I was still feeling guilty. If we could forget your mother, maybe I could forget what I had done to both her and Hera."

"You're being very honest." Andreas didn't sound impressed by that, just like he was stating a fact.

"It's time. I want my son's regard. Your wife is very smart and she's right I have to stop sniping at you. Even I can see that."

"I'll never be a Georgas."

"Maybe not on paper, but you will always be a Georgas to me." With that, Andreas's father patted him on the shoulder and walked away.

Andreas turned Kayla to face him, his expression bemused. "I didn't expect that."

"I did."

"Oh, really?"

"It's all a matter of choices, Andreas. He chose to set his pride aside to keep you in his life."

Andreas made a dismissive gesture. "I realized when we were talking that if he walked away, it wouldn't matter. I have *nothing* to prove to him. I have nothing to prove to anyone. I am who I am."

"You are." She felt the tears prickling again. "You arc an amazing man, who I love very much."

He brushed the teardrop that had formed on her eyelashes away with a gentle swipe. "My sweet Kay-love. Have I told you how beautiful you look?"

"Only about five times, including one at that altar." Still, hearing it filled her with pleasure.

"My father doesn't understand your value."

"But you do?" she teased.

"You know I do."

She nodded, so many things making sense. "The reason you didn't understand that KJ Software was my home was because I have been *your* home for six years."

"As long as you were in my life, I was okay." He leaned down and kissed her, his lips demanding and tender at the same time. He lifted his mouth from hers and spoke against her lips. "I assumed it was the same for you."

"It was, and then you broke up with me."

He straightened, but did not release her. "You didn't understand why I did it."

"I don't think you understood why you did it."

"There was only one way I could see to keep you close, connected to me." He'd said that before, but she knew now it wasn't the whole story.

She reached up and kissed him, then said, "You were afraid of what you felt for me, but you didn't want to let me go."

"I had a plan, and marriage wasn't part of it six years ago."

"Neither was falling in love."

"Neither was falling in love," he agreed.

"But you did." She waited with bated breath for his assent. No matter what she thought she knew, he had to say it.

Andreas wrapped his arms fully around her, pulling her body flush with his, her chiffon skirts floating around his legs. His gaze met hers, darkened to emerald with emotion. "I did. I loved you six years ago."

"But you thought love would make you weak."

"I discovered something when you went haring off to New York."

"Yes?"

"It wasn't love that made me weak, it was the possibility of losing you."

"That's not what you said."

"I'm stubborn."

She leaned into him. "But in love."

"Very much in love."

"Your father isn't the only one come over with honesty today."

"Maybe his submission of pride made me realize it was time I did the same."

"So, only pride kept you from admitting you love me?" She didn't believe it.

The man was arrogant, but he would never hurt her for the sake of his pride.

"I was afraid. I've only loved one other person and I lost her."

His mom. "You aren't going to lose me. We just promised each other forever."

"Losing my mom to cancer taught me that there is no

forever, or even certainty of decades." His words were cynical, but his hold on her spoke of his desire to keep Kayla close…forever.

"Our souls are entwined, Andreas. Even death cannot separate us."

His smile was magical. "Some might think that a maudlin sentiment."

"But not you?" She pressed her hand against his heart, warmed by the steady beat.

"No, not me." He leaned down and gave her another of those amazing kisses before speaking again. "I love you, my wife, my Kayla, my partner, my friend."

"I love you too, Andreas, with my whole heart."

"Forever won't be long enough."

After a thoroughly satisfying kiss that ended with the wedding guests clapping and calling out encouragement, Andreas spoke again. "No, forever won't be long enough."

And she agreed.

* * * * *

If you enjoyed
KOSTAS'S CONVENIENT BRIDE,
why not explore these other stories
by Lucy Monroe?

A VIRGIN FOR HIS PRIZE
AN HEIRESS FOR HIS EMPIRE
SHEIKH'S SCANDAL
MILLION DOLLAR CHRISTMAS PROPOSAL

Available now!

#3629 BLACKMAILED BY THE GREEK'S VOWS
Conveniently Wed!
by Tara Pammi

Discovering her passionate marriage was a business deal devastated Valentina. Yet before granting a divorce, Kairos demands she play his wife again. And soon their intense fire is reignited...

#3630 A DIAMOND DEAL WITH HER BOSS
by Cathy Williams

While pretending to be her sexy boss Gabriel's fiancée, Abby can't resist the temptation of a burning-hot affair. But soon Abby must decide: Can she share her body—*and* soul—with Gabriel?

#3631 THE SHEIKH'S SHOCK CHILD
One Night With Consequences
by Susan Stephens

When innocent laundress Millie succumbs to Sheikh Khalid's touch, she's overwhelmed by the intensity of their encounter. But becoming Khalid's mistress isn't the only consequence of their reckless desire...and Millie's scandalous news will bind them permanently!

#3632 CLAIMING HIS PREGNANT INNOCENT
by Maggie Cox

Lily doesn't expect her landlord to be gorgeous billionaire Bastian. Antagonism leads to a sensual encounter, and shocking consequences! They'll meet at the altar, but will a ring truly make Lily his?

Get 2 Free Books,
Plus 2 Free Gifts—

just for trying the Reader Service!

HP17R3

*When desert prince Dal's convenient bride is stolen,
he must find a replacement—immediately. Suddenly,
his shy secretary, Poppy, has been whisked away to
Dal's kingdom, Jolie...where she'll find herself tempted
by his expert seduction!*

Read on for a sneak preview of
Jane Porter's *next story*
KIDNAPPED FOR HIS ROYAL DUTY,
part of the **STOLEN BRIDES** *miniseries.*

Before they came to Jolie, Dal would have described
Poppy as pretty, in a fresh, wholesome, no-nonsense sort
of way with her thick, shoulder-length brown hair, large
brown eyes and serious little chin.

But as Poppy entered the dining room, with its glossy
white ceiling and dark purple walls, she looked anything
but wholesome and no-nonsense.

She was wearing a silk gown the color of cherries,
delicately embroidered with silver threads, and instead
of her usual ponytail or chignon, her dark hair was down,
and long, elegant chandelier earrings dangled from her
ears. As she walked, the semisheer kaftan molded to her
curves.

"It seems I've been keeping you waiting," she said,
her voice pitched lower than usual and slightly breathless.
"Izba insisted on all this," she added, gesturing up toward
her face.

At first Dal thought she was referring to the ornate silver earrings that were catching and reflecting the light, but once she was seated across from him, he realized her eyes had been rimmed with kohl and her lips had been outlined and filled in with a soft plum-pink gloss. "You're wearing makeup."

"Quite a lot of it, too." She grimaced. "I tried to explain to Izba that this wasn't me, but she's very determined once she makes her mind up about something and apparently, dinner with you requires me to look like a tart."

Dal checked his smile. "You don't look like a tart. Unless it's the kind of tart one wants to eat."

Color flooded Poppy's cheeks and she glanced away, suddenly shy, and he didn't know if it was her shyness or the shimmering dress that clung to her, but he didn't think any woman could be more beautiful or desirable than Poppy right now. "You look lovely," he said quietly. "But I don't want you uncomfortable all through dinner. If you'd rather go remove the makeup, I'm happy to wait."

She looked at him closely, as if doubting his sincerity. "It's fun to dress up, but I'm worried Izba has the wrong idea about me."

"And what is that?"

"She seems to think you're going to…marry…me."

Don't miss
KIDNAPPED FOR HIS ROYAL DUTY
available June 2018.

And look for the second part of the **STOLEN BRIDES** *duet,*
THE BRIDE'S BABY OF SHAME by Caitlin Crews,
available July 2018 wherever
Harlequin Presents® books and ebooks are sold.

www.Harlequin.com